FALLOUT

Todd Strasser

CANDLEWICK PRESS

Copyright © 2013 by Todd Strasser

Photograph on page 260 courtesy of the author

First paperback edition 2015

Library of Congress Catalog Card Number 2012955123
ISBN 978-0-7636-5534-1 (hardcover)
ISBN 978-0-7636-7676-6 (paperback)

18 19 20 BVG 10 9 8 7 6

Printed in Berryville, VA, U.S.A.

This book was typeset in Cambria.

Candlewick Press
99 Dover Street
Somerville, Massachusetts 02144

visit us at www.candlewick.com

For My Father

It is insane that two men, sitting on opposite sides of the world, should be able to decide to bring an end to civilization.

—JOHN F. KENNEDY
on the Cuban Missile Crisis,
October 27, 1962

1

I wake to a hand on my shoulder. Dad's voice is urgent. "Get up, Scott!" The light in the bedroom is on, and I squint up into his face. Dad's eyes are wide, and he's shaking me hard, not gently, the way he usually does when he wants to wake me.

"Up! Now!"

I rub my eyes. An inner clock tells me that it's the middle of the night. My heart starts to race with alarm. "What . . . ?"

"We're being attacked." He swivels to my little brother Sparky's bed. "Edward!"

Attacked? As my brain claws toward alertness, I hear sirens wailing in the distance. Not the melodic bursts of code directing volunteer firemen to a fire. These are shrill swooping wails.

Sparky groans and tries to roll over. Instead of arguing, Dad scoops him up, blankets and all. "Put me down!" Still half asleep, Sparky kicks as Dad cradles him and turns to me.

"Come on!"

Barefoot, heart heaving with panic, I race after him out onto the cold hall tiles, where we nearly crash into Mom, who's carrying an armful of things she's just gotten from the kitchen.

"Hurry!" Dad barks, and we scurry down the hall. In the dark playroom, he opens the closet and, with a loud clatter, sweeps away whatever toys and games lie on top of the square metal trapdoor. Outside, the sirens continue to blare.

"What's going on?" Sparky cries, awake now.

Mom dumps the things from the kitchen on the floor and pulls him close. "It's okay. Don't be scared."

But now loud banging sounds echo down the hall from the front of the house.

I gasp. "What's that?"

Without answering, Dad yanks the metal trapdoor up and points down into the square of darkness. "Go!"

I can't see a thing. "How?"

Crash! Glass smashes somewhere in the house.

"What's happening?" Sparky wails.

"It's okay," Mom says soothingly. Then to Dad: "Hurry!"

I feel Dad's arms pick me up and lower me into the emptiness. My feet dangle in the dark air. Frightened that he's about to let go, I dig my hands into his arms. "I can't see!"

"Feel the rungs with your feet!" he commands.

I find a cold metal bar with my toes just as footsteps slap into the playroom. It's Janet, our maid who stays over one night a week. She's pulling a light-blue robe closed, and her eyes are moons of terror.

"Go down!" Dad barks at me.

"Richard?" From somewhere in the house, a man's voice calls through the dark.

The metal rungs hurt the bottoms of my bare feet as I lower myself. The dark air in the shelter is cool and damp and smells like mildew. Suddenly boxes and bags of things shower down, bouncing off my head and arms, and falling into the shadows below. I cry out in surprise, even though it doesn't really hurt. Already Mom's feet are on the rungs just above me.

"Hurry!" Dad yells.

"Ow!" Sparky cries, and I wonder if Dad accidentally banged him into something as he tried to lower him through the trapdoor.

One of my feet touches the cold concrete floor; the other steps on a box that collapses with a crunch.

"In there!" a man's voice shouts.

Above me, Mom yells, "Careful, Edward!"

Suddenly there's scratching and grunting overhead. Sparky cries out, and Mom gasps loudly. Something big is plummeting down, and I barely have time to jump out of the way before Mom crashes to the floor with a horrible, crunching thud, Sparky on her chest.

"Mom!" A terrified cry tears through my throat. "Sparky!"

two

"Me could eat horse, Kemo Sabe," Freak O' Nature said in the diction of Tonto, the Lone Ranger's Indian sidekick. Freak O' Nature's real name was Norman Freeman, but his friends called him Freak O' Nature because . . . well, because that's what he was.

It was the last week of fifth grade, and he, Ronnie, and I were lounging on his lawn listening to Freak O' Nature's black transistor radio, which lay on the grass broadcasting the game between the Yankees and the Cleveland Indians. Mickey Mantle, playing for the first time after a month on the disabled list, had just smashed a come-from-behind pinch-hit home run to put the Yanks ahead 9–7.

"Who wants to bet they still lose?" asked Ronnie, wearing a colorful Indian madras short-sleeve shirt that was the current height of style.

"Me hungry," said Freak O' Nature, who sat cross-legged, all sharp, bony angles, with brown hair, freckles, and thin metal wires across his upper and lower teeth from his bite plates.

Lying on my back, feeling the grass tickle my neck and ears, I gazed up at the puffy white clouds in the blue sky. The June sun warmed our faces and arms. In a few days, school would end, and we would have all summer to play baseball and swim and have fun.

On the radio, the Indians' pitcher Gary Bell got Clete Boyer out on a ground ball and Bobby Richardson swinging. But it didn't matter. The Mick was back, and the Yanks were winning.

"Want a Sara Lee cheesecake?" Ronnie asked as he sucked on a stem of clover he'd plucked from the lawn. He was a stocky, muscular kid with black hair greased back along the sides of his head into a ducktail, while the front hung down in a spit curl.

The thought of sweet, creamy cheese filling and graham-cracker crust made my stomach rumble with anticipation. Even though it was only an hour before dinnertime and a sure bet to ruin my appetite, I asked, "How?"

"There's a million of 'em in Linda's garage."

Ronnie might have been exaggerating, but we got the point. The houses in our neighborhood didn't have basements, so people put freezers in their garages and filled them with food.

"You mean, steal it?" I sat up and tugged nervously at the hair behind my ear. I'd never stolen anything . . . except for the stuff it was okay to steal, like cookies from the kitchen when Mom wasn't around and our Halloween candy from the shopping bag Dad hid in his closet so Sparky and I wouldn't eat it all at once — but really, we suspected, so he could eat some of it, too.

"It's not stealing," Ronnie insisted. "We know Linda. Besides, you ever looked in their freezer? It's so full, they'll never notice if one cheesecake is gone."

Linda Lewandowski had four brothers and sisters, so it made sense that there might be more food in the freezer than her mother could keep track of. But even if there'd been enough cheesecakes to fill Yankee Stadium, that still didn't make stealing right.

Freak O' Nature gave me an uncertain look. "What you think, Kemo Scott?"

"What if we get caught?" I asked.

Ronnie plucked another clover from the lawn and sucked on it pensively. "What difference will it make? We could all be dead tomorrow."

3

From above come grunts, banging, and scraping — the sounds of a scuffle. "Richard, let us in!" someone shouts frantically. "Don't let us die!"

Petrified with fear, I crouch on the concrete floor beside Janet, who climbed down after Mom fell. The still forms of Mom and Sparky lie in the dark while Dad clings to the metal rungs and tries to pull the trapdoor closed. But people on the other side are trying to pull it open.

The light's gone on in the playroom, and the shelter brightens each time the trapdoor rises a few inches, then darkens again when Dad manages to yank it down. With each flash of light, I glimpse Mom on her back, one arm stretched out, one leg bent at the knee, the other propped against the wall, Sparky sprawled on top of her.

My brother begins to whimper. Janet draws him off Mom and into her arms. I can't tell if he's hurt, but at least he's moving and making sounds. Unlike Mom, who lies perfectly still.

The trapdoor rises enough to let in the wail of sirens. Someone shouts a curse. Dad's feet are wedged into the metal rungs. His teeth are gritted with exertion as he struggles to close the door. I want to beg him to let the others in. But I don't because this is something I've been scared of ever since he first told me about the shelter, since I realized we were the only family on the block who had one. What if there are dozens of people up there? What if more are coming? What if they all try to squeeze in until those of us at the bottom are crushed to death?

The trapdoor rises. A thin metal tube slides in and swings around as if trying to hit Dad's arms and break his grip. It's a pole from the badminton net.

"Scott, the rope!" Dad shouts.

My eyes meet Janet's. "Do what he says," she tells me.

I look up at Dad. "Where?"

"On the wall!"

We're in a narrow corridor lined with cinder blocks. From a previous visit down here, I know that the wall he's talking about is around the corner, in the shelter itself.

But the small amounts of light seeping in from above don't reach that far. "I can't see!" I yell.

"The light!" Dad shouts. "On the string from the ceiling!"

I scuttle into the pitch-black shelter. Stopping in what I think should be the center of the room, I wave my arms around until I feel a string and pull. A lightbulb bursts on, and in the glare I see the kitty-corner double-decker bunks and wooden shelves lined with food and other supplies. On the wall, a coiled rope is looped over a hook. I grab it. Back out in the narrow corridor, Janet is comforting Sparky, who's staring fearfully up while Dad struggles. Mom still hasn't moved. Something dark is pooling under her head.

A tennis racket slides through the gap between the trapdoor and the closet floor. They're using it as a lever to pry the door open. Dad reaches down and grabs the coil of rope from my hands. Now, in addition to the badminton pole and tennis racket, fingers appear along the edge of the trapdoor. First a few, then more and more, turning white around the fingernails as they strain to pull upward.

The trapdoor starts to rise. The rope falls to the floor beside Mom as Dad tightens his grip on the latch. He grits his teeth and struggles, but the hands from above pull the door higher, and through the gap I see bare feet, pajama-clad legs, the hems of robes . . . then faces peering in — tight lips and clenched teeth like Dad's. The door rises another inch. Dad is being stretched, the skin of his stomach showing between his pajama top and bottoms.

"Uhhh!" he grunts, and lets go.

The trapdoor flies open and light spills in, accompanied by yelps and thuds as the people who were pulling fall backward. The badminton pole and tennis racket tumble down on us with dull thunks. Janet and Sparky cower. Mom doesn't react. Familiar faces crowd around the square opening above. Ronnie and his father. Mr. McGovern and Paula . . .

Clinging to the rungs in the wall, Dad gapes up at them. "There's no room," he protests meekly.

The faces grow determined and grim.

"Go down, Ronnie!" Mr. Shaw shouts.

"But Scott's dad said —"

"Go!" Mr. Shaw yells.

Ronnie's bare foot feels for the top rung. Dad reaches up and swats at it.

"He's stopping me!" Ronnie cries.

Ronnie's feet rise as if he's flying away. They're replaced by bigger feet. Dad swipes at them, but the feet kick back. Legs in blue pajamas force Dad down the rungs.

"You'll kill us all!" he protests.

Ronnie's dad answers with a curse and takes another step down.

"Watch out for Mom!" I cry at Dad, who momentarily freezes when he sees her crumpled below.

Meanwhile, Mr. Shaw and Ronnie are coming down, while others crowd around the trapdoor waiting their turn. Dad hops from the bottom rung, trying not to step on Mom.

"Get her into the shelter!" he yells at Janet as he quickly slides his hands under Mom's shoulders. Janet grabs Mom's ankles, and together they maneuver her around the shield wall. Sparky runs into my arms, his heart beating as fast as a hamster's as we follow Dad and Janet. My last glimpse is of Mr. Shaw helping Ronnie off the rungs while more people climb down. The nightmare is coming true. We're going to be crushed.

four

You never knew what might come out of Ronnie's mouth, but on that June afternoon, our heads filled with baseball and cheesecake, the suggestion that we could all be dead tomorrow was unexpectedly jarring.

"What are you talking about?" Freak O' Nature asked him in a normal voice.

"Nuclear war," I said, since that was the only thing that could result in all three of us being dead by the morning. All year long, the Communist threat had been growing as the Russians spread their influence in Asia and South America and even to a little country called Cuba, which was an island somewhere south of Florida ruled by a

Commie named Castro who had a scruffy beard, wore a green army uniform, and smoked cigars.

"My dad heard the Ruskies are sending ships filled with fighter jets, bombers, and missiles to Cuba," Ronnie said. "And if we try to stop them, it'll be war."

The Russians were evil. Their chubby bald-headed leader, Nikita Khrushchev, had crooked teeth and an ugly gap between the front two, which showed that Russians didn't even believe in orthodontia. And if that didn't make him anti-American enough, there was the time he'd come to the United Nations and banged his shoe on the rostrum, which proved beyond a doubt that the Commies were unpredictable, violent, and crazy enough to blow us all up.

Clover stem squeezed between his lips, Ronnie pushed himself up to his feet and reached down, offering me his hand. "Come on, let's eat."

I felt my stomach tighten at the thought of the proposed criminal enterprise.

"Well?" Ronnie's hand was still out. I grabbed it, just like always.

Freak O' Nature scooped up the transistor radio and sprang to his feet. He was the only kid we knew who could go from sitting Indian style to standing without using his hands, this being one more piece of evidence of his general freak o' naturedness.

We walked along the sidewalk past our neighbors'

homes, each on a quarter acre of property with a front lawn just large enough for a bunch of eleven-year-old boys to play touch football.

As the three of us neared Linda's house, I couldn't help wondering how Ronnie expected to get a cheesecake out of the freezer without one of the numerous Lewandowski children, or Mrs. Lewandowski herself, catching us.

Relief washed through me when the Lewandowskis' garage came into view. "It's closed," I announced, trying not to let on how much better I felt now that I wouldn't have to help Ronnie steal.

"Because they're not home," said Ronnie. "Linda told me she was going to the doctor this afternoon."

The Lewandowskis had a station wagon, and whenever Mrs. Lewandowski took one of her kids somewhere, all the others had to go as well. It was not unusual to see their car weaving erratically down the street, Mrs. Lewandowski steering with her left hand while reaching back to smack one misbehaving child or another with her right.

"So . . . what're we gonna do?" I bit my lower lip nervously.

"Go in there and get us a cheesecake," Ronnie replied, as if the answer were obvious. He stopped at the end of the Lewandowskis' driveway and gazed at the house, which was the color of chocolate pudding.

My queasiness leaped up a notch; intentionally

opening a garage door seemed to imply a greater degree of juvenile delinquency than merely wandering in. I reached behind my ear and took hold of a few more hairs. "You mean, open the garage door?"

"No, Scott, I'm going to walk right through it like that scientist in *4D Man*."

"Nothing can stop him," Freak O' Nature said in a deep ominous voice, quoting from the TV commercial currently promoting the movie. "A man in the fourth dimension is in . . . de . . . struc . . . ti . . . ble."

By now my reluctance had risen to the level of near-paralysis. "You sure about this?"

"What's the big deal?" Ronnie asked impatiently. "The Lewandowskis are our neighbors. We share stuff all the time."

"But we ask first," I said.

"If they were here, I'd ask." Ronnie took a few steps up the driveway, then stopped and looked back at us. "You guys aren't *chicken,* are you?"

5

Leaving a smudged trail of blood on the concrete floor, Dad and Janet get Mom to a bunk. Ronnie and Mr. Shaw, in their pajamas, stumble into the shelter and look around. Mrs. Shaw, in a pink bathrobe, arrives next. From around the shield wall come shouts of people urging each other to hurry and go down.

Dad spins to face Mr. Shaw. "We're all going to die," he growls as Paula comes in with tears running down her face. "There're already too many. There won't be enough food or water for all of us."

Mr. Shaw and my father face each other for an instant, then march back around the shield wall. Meanwhile

Sparky's still holding on to me, and I can't stop looking at Mom, now cradled in Janet's arms, and wishing she'd move. Ronnie and Paula also stare. Mrs. Shaw pulls both of them to her.

On the other side of the shield wall, Dad and Mr. Shaw shout that there are too many people. Loud grunts and curses follow, as if there's a fight. A man shouts, "My daughter's in there!" In the shelter, Paula cries out, "Daddy!" Her sobs grow louder, and Mrs. Shaw hugs her and says it's going to be okay. But that can't be true. There's a nuclear war and Mom's bleeding and too many people are already in the shelter and more are trying to get in.

The fighting and yelling grow louder. Sparky's grip on me tightens as he pleads, "Make it stop!"

Mr. McGovern staggers around the shield wall with a long red scratch across his cheek. Paula breaks away from Mrs. Shaw, but before she gets to him, there's a sudden bright flash of light as if someone on the other side of the shield wall took a photograph.

A woman's scream pierces the air.

The bulb in the ceiling goes out.

Everything turns dark.

The sirens in the distance stop.

"What happened?" Sparky asks anxiously in the inky void.

Clang! On the other side of the shield wall, the

trapdoor slams shut, and I hear a clank as if a bolt has been thrown.

It is pitch-black in the shelter.

The momentary silence is broken by Paula's sobs, then into the darkness come ragged breaths — Dad's and Mr. Shaw's. From around the shield wall come thuds of fists drumming against the trapdoor. A muffled female voice cries hysterically, "Richard! Richard!"

It's horrible. I cover my ears, but it doesn't help. More thuds and frantic begging join in. "Please!" "For the love of God!" "Don't let us die!"

"I'm scared!" Sparky wails. In the blackness, his sobs join Paula's.

"Don't listen," Mrs. Shaw gasps, as if such a thing might be possible.

Despite the panicked shouts coming from the other side of the trapdoor, there is a strange stillness in the shelter.

"Scott?" Dad says somberly somewhere in the dark.

"Dad?" Ronnie says at the same time his mother says, "Steven?"

"I'm here," Mr. Shaw answers, breathing heavily.

Loud clanks and thumps fill our ears as those left above beat at the trapdoor. But it is made of quarter-inch iron plate. Nothing short of a bazooka could blast through it.

"Make it stop," Sparky pleads.

But it doesn't. There's no getting away from the agonized cries of those who've been locked out. Stomach cramped, heart racing, I fight back tears and wish the banging and shouting would go away.

Now there's a new, more distant sound . . . growing steadily louder like thunder. Then a roar, and one last awful scream that disappears into deafening clatter and crashing. In the dark below, I cower over Sparky and imagine something like a tornado above obliterating everything in its path.

It rumbles over us, followed by a few muffled thumps.

And then . . . quiet.

SIX

"Keep an eye out," Ronnie told Freak O' Nature, and continued up the Lewandowskis' driveway. Feeling lightheaded with misgivings, I followed, wondering if Ronnie felt that way, too. He had to know that stealing was wrong. Was a Sara Lee frozen cheesecake really worth this much anxiety?

At the garage door, I glanced back at Freak O' Nature, hoping he would signal that someone was coming and we should abandon this unlawful endeavor. But he wasn't even looking at us. Instead he was staring down at his radio as if watching the words come out.

Ronnie took hold of the garage-door handle. The door creaked upward, revealing a shadowy interior that smelled of car oil and dry grass and was crammed with bicycles, toy carriages, and Hula-Hoops. Without a word, he marched toward the back. The freezer was one of those horizontal models, and a small cloud of chilled white vapor rose into our faces when Ronnie lifted the top. The inner walls were caked white with ice, and it was filled with rectangular packages of chicken pot pies, frozen vegetables, Swanson TV dinners, and the treasure that we sought, Sara Lee frozen cheesecakes. Ronnie picked up a box, covered with a thin film of ice crystals.

And that's when the Lewandowskis' station wagon pulled in.

7

"Turn on a light!" Sparky sobs. Paula's still crying, too. It's impossibly dark.

"Give me a moment," Dad says wearily, his words interrupted by deep breaths.

Above us, there's only silence, as if the world has stopped.

Or disappeared.

"*Please,* Dad?" Sparky implores.

"Yes, Edward," Dad answers in his soft voice. There's a faint rustle in the blackness as he feels around for a light.

"Mom?" I say.

She doesn't answer. I wonder if Janet's still holding her. I'd give anything to hear her reassuring voice.

Paula continues to sob in the dark. It's just her and her dad. Not her mom or brother. My stomach twists. I hate to think of what's happened to them. Our mom may be hurt, but at least she's here.

There's a soft slithering sound like Dad sliding his hands along the wall. "Everybody be still," he says. "There's a flashlight around here somewhere."

Clinks and scratching follow, as if he's touching things.

Crash!

People cry out in surprise. For one terrifying instant, I imagine that the roof of the shelter is caving in, then realize it was just a bunch of things falling from a shelf. Dad curses, then says, "Sorry, everyone."

"You all right?" Mr. Shaw asks.

"Yes."

"Dad, *please* turn on a light," Sparky begs.

"I'm trying, Edward. Believe me, I'm trying." There's frustration in his voice. Things jangle and scrape as he sorts through whatever fell.

"What about the light from before?" Sparky asks.

I don't want Dad to get angry, which he sometimes does when we ask too many questions. So I tell Sparky, "It won't work. There's no electricity anymore."

"Why not?"

There's a clunk and Dad grunts, "Damn it!" as if he banged his head.

"Are you okay?" This time it's Mrs. Shaw who asks.

"Yes." But he sounds even more frustrated. Sometimes when he got this way in the house, I would hide in a closet.

"Why isn't there electricity?" Sparky asks.

"Because the bomb blew everything up," I tell him.

"I didn't hear a bomb," my brother says.

"Be quiet," Dad snaps. "I'm trying to think."

"But I didn't hear a bomb," Sparky whines, his voice breaking. "Just turn on the light."

"Quiet!" Dad bellows.

Sparky starts crying again. Fearing Dad will get angrier and yell even more, I pull my brother tighter to me and shush him the way Mom would. More clinking and scratching follows. Then, finally, a click and a light goes on.

It takes a moment for my eyes to adjust, then I see Dad near the bunks, shining the beam from a long silver flashlight on Mom, whose head is on Janet's lap. My breath catches; there's a big red stain on Janet's robe. Mom's hair is dark and gummy, and in the dim light her skin looks almost gray.

"Mom!" Sparky wails rawly. He bursts out of my grasp and flies toward her, but Dad catches him.

"She's going to be okay," he says, swinging the flashlight beam away. I bite my tongue not to say what I'm thinking, which is that she doesn't look like she's going to be okay. Dad has to wrestle Sparky, who's still struggling to get to Mom. "We have to leave her alone, Edward," he says softly. "We have to let her get better." He holds my little brother gently but firmly.

"Listen to your father," Janet tells him.

"But what's wrong with her?" Sparky asks anxiously, craning to see around Dad.

"Mr. Porter, is there a first-aid kit?" Janet asks.

Dad aims the flashlight at some shelves. "Get it, Scott."

I rise, and that's when I notice Mr. McGovern and Paula near the shield wall. Paula's curled in his arms and weeping miserably. Mr. McGovern hugs her, his eyes glistening.

They're half a family.

It's . . . horrible.

eight

"Run!" Ronnie yelled.

We sprinted around the Lewandowskis' station wagon — past the astonished faces of Mrs. Lewandowski, Linda, and the rest of the brood — and out into the sunlight, where there was no sign of Freak O' Nature. I didn't understand why we were running. Mrs. Lewandowski had seen us. Lest there be any doubt, she now stood at the mouth of the garage and called, "Ronnie? Scott? What's going on?"

Being a dutiful child who'd been taught to answer grown-ups, I began to slow, but Ronnie grunted, "Don't stop!"

So I sped up again.

With the cheesecake box tucked into the crook of his arm like a football, Ronnie led the way. On the sidewalk ahead of us was Freak O' Nature, who'd abandoned his lookout post and was walking home with the transistor radio pressed to his ear. For a moment, I wondered if Ronnie was running after him, angry that Freak O' Nature had gone AWOL. But he ran right past him and kept going.

As I sprinted past Freak O' Nature, he asked, "Where're you going?"

"We got caught!" I gasped.

Ronnie ran another hundred yards and then slowed to a jog. I would have gained on him, but I was winded and slowing as well. Soon we were walking about fifteen yards apart. A stitch had started to cramp in my right side.

"Wait." I gulped in pain. "She saw us. She called our names."

But Ronnie kept going — down the sidewalk . . . across Freak O' Nature's front yard . . . around the side of his house . . . and into the backyard, where he plopped down under a maple tree. I flopped down opposite him, massaging the stitch in my side.

Neither of us spoke. Ronnie sat staring at the Sara Lee cheesecake box in his lap.

A minute later, Freak O' Nature joined us, dropping into an Indian-style position.

"Thanks a lot," Ronnie growled.

"For what?" asked Freak O' Nature.

"I told you to keep an eye out."

"I did."

"For the *Lewandowskis*."

"Oh." Freak O' Nature mulled this over. "Sorry."

"She's probably telling our mothers right now." I imagined Mrs. Lewandowski on the party line, reporting the incident to both our moms at once. "We're dead."

"You could give it back," suggested Freak O' Nature.

"No!" Ronnie clutched the box as if it would shoot right back to the freezer if he let go.

"It's just a stupid cheesecake," I said.

To end the debate, Ronnie tore open the box and peeled back the round tinfoil lid, revealing the light-brown-rimmed yellow cake inside. I wished I felt hungry, but mostly I felt dread. Getting caught stealing surely qualified as a spankable offense.

Prying the cake out, Ronnie gripped the sides and tried to break off a piece, but in its frozen state, it wouldn't even bend. He bared his teeth in the effort, then finally smashed the cake against his knee. It broke sort of in half, and he handed the smaller piece to me and kept the larger for himself.

"What about me?" Freak O' Nature asked.

"You abandoned your post," Ronnie said.

Freak O' Nature didn't reply. He rarely argued with anyone.

The chunk Ronnie had given me bore the indentations of his fingers and was covered with his fingerprints. Ronnie bit into the corner of his piece where the filling met the graham-cracker crust. He held the bite in his mouth for a moment, probably letting the cheesecake soften, and then closed his eyes, a blissful smile appearing on his lips as if to rub in Freak O' Nature's loss.

Somehow, despite all the regret I felt about my participation in this terrible crime, and the apprehension about being punished, my appetite crept back. I found a corner of cake free of Ronnie's fingerprints and took a nibble. The cheesecake was cold and creamy and delicious, and I bit off a little of the nutty brown crust to go along with it. Like a prisoner on death row, I began to savor my last meal.

9

The medical kit is the size of a lunch box, with a red cross on it. Next to it is a green box I've seen once before, in Dad's closet. I know what's in that box, and finding it here catches me by surprise and makes me uncomfortable. I look away and take the first-aid kit to Dad.

He hands me the flashlight. "Keep it aimed on her."

I shine the beam at Mom's face, which is gray with some black-and-blue marks near her ears. As Dad rips open a gauze pad, then gently lifts Mom's head and presses the pad against the wound, my stomach coils with anxiety. Her hair in back is all dark reddish and stuck together. As if Dad knows what I'm thinking, he says, "It looks bad, but head wounds bleed a lot."

"Uh-huh." I agree, mostly because I don't want him to get mad.

"We'll just have to wait until she wakes up," he says, holding the gauze pad in place and pulling a long strip of white tape, which he starts to wrap around her head.

"Mr. Porter?" Janet says.

"Yes?" Dad looks up.

"That's not the way."

Their eyes meet for a moment, and then Dad nods and lets her take over.

Janet takes a small pair of scissors from the first-aid kit and begins to cut the hair away from Mom's wound.

No one speaks. The *snip, snip, snip* of the scissors is the only sound in this little cement box of a room. Maybe there's too much to think about. Paula and her dad must be thinking about Mrs. McGovern and Teddy. Is Ronnie thinking about his collie, Leader? What about the rest of our friends and neighbors, teachers, cousins, and grand-parents? Did some of them find shelter in basements and tunnels and the other places with those black-and-yellow Civil Defense Fallout Shelter signs?

Maybe some, but not *everybody.* Not the ones who were on the other side of the trapdoor.

Huddled in the shadows with her husband and Ronnie, Mrs. Shaw quietly begins to sob.

Snip, snip, snip . . . Dark clumps of hair fall to the concrete floor. Janet turns to Dad. "Could I have some water, Mr. Porter?"

With a start, Dad snatches the flashlight from me and shines it up at a large red sausage-shaped metal tank hanging above us. Skinny brown pipes run into it from the ceiling. Rising quickly, he reaches up and turns some valves, then waits as if he's expecting something. Everyone else looks up, too. Paula's cheeks glisten with tears.

"Come on," Dad mutters at the tank, and I feel myself tense.

Seconds pass. He stares intently. "Come on!"

I'm not sure what's supposed to happen, but it's obvious from the way Dad's acting that it's important.

"What is it?" Mr. Shaw asks.

"The water tank. I was supposed to fill it."

"It can't be too late, can it?" asks Mrs. Shaw while Dad shines the flashlight beam on a metal toolbox on the floor near the wall.

"I don't hear water running." He flips the box open, pulls out a hammer, and starts tapping the pipes. *Clank! Clank! Clank!*

Paula buries her face in her father's shoulder. Dad stops and listens, then starts to hit the pipes harder. *CLANK! CLANK! CLANK!*

Sparky covers his ears. "Stop! It's too loud."

Dad listens again. In the glow of the flashlight, the sinews tighten in his neck and his temple pulses.

CLANK! CLANK! CLANK!

Despite the jarring racket, Mom lies perfectly still.

ten

By the time we'd licked the last traces of cheesecake from our fingers, the afternoon was descending toward evening, the shadows growing longer and deeper. The distant train whistle meant fathers were coming home from work. The sweet pleasure of the cheesecake vanished, replaced by the sour taste of dread.

"The Yankees lost," Freak O' Nature said in his normal voice, not affecting any well-known television character, and looked at his watch. "I gotta go in. Are . . . you guys gonna say I had something to do with it?"

Ronnie and I looked at each other and shook our heads. School-yard logic might have dictated that since he'd been part of the crime at the beginning, he was a tiny bit culpable, but spreading the blame probably wouldn't reduce whatever punishment we would face at home.

"Thanks." With a smile of relief and gratitude, Freak O' Nature stood up. Since we were in his backyard, Ronnie and I got up as well. As we started toward our homes, the train whistle blew again, sounding closer.

"I'm gonna get it bad," I said, trying not to step on the unlucky cracks in the sidewalk—a last-ditch effort to keep things from becoming worse.

"We could all be dead tomorrow," Ronnie said.

Either way, I felt doomed.

At the front door, Sparky was waiting with an expression of awe on his face. Even though he got into plenty of trouble himself, nothing thrilled and fascinated him more than when the ax was about to fall on me. Before he could say anything, I raised my hand and said, "I know."

But he had to say it anyway. "You're in big trouble." He grinned with delight.

Mom came out of the kitchen wearing a blue apron and a frown on her face. Then she spoke the words that struck an even greater, or at least more immediate, fear than a Russian attack: "Go to your room until your father gets home."

11

Dad slumps down on the bunk kitty-corner to where Janet sits, still comforting Mom. The tension is gone. Either Dad's tired or he's decided that more banging on pipes won't help. Sparky goes over and settles on his leg. I sit next to him, pressing my shoulder against his arm. In Dad's hands, the flashlight makes a bright bull's-eye against the wall of gray concrete blocks.

"Mr. Porter?" Janet speaks softly.

Dad shines the light back on Mom. Using a bandage and some alcohol from the first-aid kit, Janet wipes her hands, then starts cutting again.

Snip, snip, snip . . .

"Everyone we know," Mrs. Shaw sniffs woefully. "Everyone!"

Mr. McGovern mutters, "It's unbelievable."

There are places I can't stop my thoughts from going to: What about the others who were up there? The ones who didn't get in? Were Paula's mom and brother among them? Freak O' Nature and his family? The Lewandowskis and Sinclairs? Were they all blinded and burned in the heat flash? Poisoned by radiation? Blown apart by the shock wave?

Or are they still out there trying to avoid the fallout floating down out of the sky like poisonous gray snow? Dad said that if you weren't in a shelter, the fallout would be unavoidable. Even if you managed not to get any on you or breathe it in, it would still get into the water and food. At the end of World War II, the United States dropped atom bombs on Hiroshima and Nagasaki in Japan, and hundreds of thousands of Japanese people died from the explosions and the radiation that followed. And those bombs were tiny compared to the hydrogen bombs that the United States and Russia have now.

Thinking of my friends brings a deep, sick, sad sensation. Freak O' Nature, Linda, Puddin' Belly Wright, and Why Can't You Be Like Johnny? could be lying on the ground above us right now, writhing in pain. Shouldn't we go up and look for them? But I know what Dad would say. We'd only be exposing ourselves to the radiation. Then we'd die, too.

Still, how would it feel if it was someone else's bomb shelter and our family were the ones who were locked out? I picture myself crawling through the rubble to the trapdoor, knocking and begging to be let in.

My lungs expand with an involuntary gasp. So far no one's knocked, but what if someone *does*?

Ronnie presses his face against his dad's arm while Mr. Shaw wipes his own eyes with his fingers. Sparky sniffs. Dad stares at the floor. Now I can't stop the tears from coming. In the past when there'd been tears in my eyes, I'd always gone to Mom for comfort. I never wanted Dad to see me cry because that was what girls and little kids did. But what does that matter now?

Janet wraps Mom's head in gauze to keep everything in place. It's so quiet. The loudest sound is Mom's breathing. Dad hardly takes his eyes off her. Every few moments, he reaches over to feel her forehead, pull her robe a little tighter, brush a few hairs away from her face.

"When's she going to wake up?" Sparky asks.

"Don't know," Dad says.

"What if she never wakes up?"

"Let's not think about that."

- - - - - - -

More time passes. More silence. Dad takes the hammer and raps the pipes again — *Clank! Clank! Clank!* — then pauses to listen.

Still nothing.

He sighs, puts down the hammer, takes some blankets from a shelf, and offers them around. "Try to make yourselves comfortable."

Janet is the only one who says thank you. The Shaws and McGoverns spread the blankets on the cold concrete floor. Both Mrs. Shaw and Paula tuck their knees up against their chests and hug their legs. Paula leans tightly against her dad. After making Mom comfortable on the bunk, Janet sits on the bare concrete floor and wraps her blanket around her shoulders. Soon we are four groups, huddled close to one another in the chilly, damp air.

In science we learned that some people could go a month or more without food by living on stored-up fat and then on muscle. But no one can go much more than four days without water.

It's Sparky who asks the question we're all thinking: "Dad, what will happen if we can't get the water?"

twelve

I went to my room, which I shared with Sparky, whose real name was Edward, but I called him Sparky because his hair grew straight out from his head as if he was always touching something electric.

Wondering how bad the spanking would be, I sat on my bed, tugging at the hair behind my ear, too miserable to look at comics or play with my plastic army men. The paddleball racket was a given. When I was younger, Dad used to spank me, and then Sparky, with his hand, but one day he hurt his wrist and couldn't play tennis for a few weeks, so now he spanked us with the wooden paddle, which hurt like the dickens.

The bedroom door began to open and I tensed, but it was only Sparky. He pretended to look for a toy on his shelf, but I knew he'd really come in to see how I was coping with the stress. He kept glancing at me out of the corner of his eye.

"Dad's really gonna give it to you. You're not supposed to steal."

"Get lost." I picked up *MAD* magazine and pretended to read it. The black and white enemies in "Spy vs. Spy" used the same round black bombs with fizzy fuses that Boris Badenov used against Rocky and Bullwinkle on TV.

"Mom says she doesn't know what she's gonna do with you."

That didn't sound right. Taking the cheesecake was the first bad thing I'd done in months. "No, she didn't."

"Yes, she did," Sparky insisted.

"Liar."

"Nuh-uh. She said, 'I don't know what I'm going to do.' And her eyes got red and watery."

That sounded ominous. Was it possible that even I didn't know how bad what I'd done was? I'd done bad stuff before, like the time Puddin' Belly Wright and I threw dirt bombs at the back of Old Lady Lester's freshly painted garage, or the time I dropped Sparky's brand-new rubber football down the storm drain because he wouldn't share his double-stick cherry ice pop.

But I'd never stolen before. Could stealing mean you'd crossed the line into juvenile delinquency and there was no going back? Could it mean I'd have to be a hood from now on and wear a leather jacket and heavy engineer boots all summer and pretend to be tough even though I knew I wasn't very tough at all? Would I be the only kid on the block who was a hood, and none of my friends would be allowed to play with me? Just thinking about it made me want to cry.

"Go away or you're gonna get hurt," I warned Sparky.

He left and I felt tears of regret slide down my cheeks. Why had I listened to Ronnie?

When the door opened a few moments later, I thought it would be Sparky again, but Dad came in, wearing a dark-green suit. I sniffed loudly, hoping he'd see my red eyes and tear-streaked cheeks and know how remorseful I was and that I'd clearly learned my lesson and therefore really didn't need to be spanked.

The good news was he didn't have the paddle, but that could have been because he wanted to change clothes before he spanked me. Dad never did work around the house in his business clothes. He always changed into dungarees and a sweatshirt first. And that included when he punished us.

I pulled my knees up under my chin and tried to squeeze a few more tears of remorse out of my eyes. Sitting across from me on Sparky's bed, Dad looked serious, his jaw dark with five o'clock shadow, which was something gangsters and men who were desperate or crazy often had on TV.

"You know you're not supposed to steal," he said.

I nodded, blinked hard, and sniffed loudly again. At the same time, I tried to estimate how many swats with the paddle I might get. The last time Dad had spanked me was after I did an experiment to see whether a little rock the size of a nickel could break a window if you threw it really hard from close up. The answer was yes, if a five-inch crack in the glass counted. That got me three swats. But that time Mom hadn't cried or said she didn't know what she was going to do with me. All she did was laugh and say, "Your father is going to love this."

So it stood to reason that the punishment for stealing would be greater — maybe even six or more swats. But it also depended on Dad's mood. If this was one of those days when he came home angry, it could be even worse.

"Why did you do it?" He sounded calm and reasonable, so I felt a little hopeful. The truth was, I didn't know why I'd done it. Hunger had played a part. And Ronnie had said I'd be a chicken if I didn't do it.

"I don't know."

"But you knew it was wrong."

I nodded and felt a tiny bit encouraged; he didn't seem all that angry.

"Do you have anything to say for yourself?" he asked.

"Ronnie said it wouldn't matter because tomorrow the Russians might drop the bomb and we'd all be dead."

To be honest, I didn't think that was such a good excuse, but it was the best I could come up with. At that point, if I'd had to estimate how many swats I was going to get once Dad changed clothes, I would have guessed around five. But Dad didn't move. He blinked, then blinked again. "Stay here," he said, then left the room.

13

"Is there any water at all?" Mrs. Shaw asks. In the dim light, her eyes are glittery.

Dad shakes his head.

"And if we go up there to get some . . . ?"

"We have to wait as long as we can before leaving the shelter," Dad says.

"Maybe it's not as bad as you think," Mr. McGovern suggests.

"A bomb went off close by," Dad says. "We saw the flash and heard the blast winds."

"But we don't *really* know," Paula's dad stresses.

Dad glances at Mom again. On her cheek are a few

streaks of dark dried blood. "I'll check the levels." He takes the flashlight and gets up.

"Can I come?" Sparky asks anxiously.

"No, it could be dangerous."

I put my arm around Sparky's scrawny shoulders. "We'll stay here."

Dad gets a small box labeled FAMILY RADIATION MEASUREMENT KIT. Inside is a tubelike thing about the size of a fountain pen. He goes around the shield wall and into the narrow corridor on the other side.

Without the flashlight, it gets darker in the shelter. We watch the shadows and light in the gap where the shield wall ends and listen as Dad climbs the metal rungs up to the trapdoor.

A few moments later, he returns. "It's four hundred ninety-seven roentgens under the door. That's what's getting *through* a quarter inch of iron plate, which means it's even worse on the other side."

"What does that mean?" asks Mrs. Shaw.

"Anything over fifty roentgens will cause radiation sickness. Anyone who goes out there will be sick within hours and dead within days."

fourteen

When Dad came back into the bedroom, he was still wearing his suit and wasn't carrying the paddle. "We're going to the Lewandowskis.'"

"Noooo!" I wailed, instantly filled with a different sort of dread; the only thing worse than physical pain was the pain of embarrassment. Now I knew where he'd gone when he left the room — to call Mrs. Lewandowski.

"Yes," Dad said firmly. "I want you to apologize."

"Can't I call?"

"In person." Dad's tone invited no more arguing.

This was the worst, most humiliating thing ever. Not only because I'd have to apologize to Mrs. Lewandowski, but because Linda was pretty and blond . . . and I had a crush on her that was so secret even Russian torturers wouldn't have been able to beat it out of me. Just being near her made me nervous and tongue-tied. The thought of going over there to apologize was unbearable.

"How about you just spank me?" I begged.

Dad's mouth fell open. "Are . . . you serious?"

I nodded. A spanking would hurt more, but once it was over, you forgot about it. But I saw Linda every day in school. If I did what Dad wanted me to do, I was doomed to a lifetime of embarrassment.

15

Dad takes a radio from the shelf and sits down with Sparky and me. He turns the dials. Between gaps of nothing come static and noises like sound bending. He goes back to the static and fiddles around, but all he gets is crackling, scratchy noise.

"What about the Civil Defense channel?" Mr. McGovern asks.

"Tried it." Dad turns the dial. There's nothing. How can this be a war? No explosions. No shots being fired. Not a sound from above.

After he snaps the radio off, it's silent except for Paula's sniffs. It feels like a long time has passed, but it can't be more than an hour or two since Dad picked up Sparky and carried him down the hall to the playroom. Sparky yawns and rubs his eyes. I can't believe he's actually sleepy. Maybe he's too young to really understand what's happened.

So far Ronnie and I have avoided looking at each other. Last night, just a few hours before Dad shook me awake, Ronnie and I had the first fistfight of our lives. It happened on the way back from having birthday cake at Why Can't You Be Like Johnny?'s house, and now I don't know whether to still be angry at him or just try to forget. It seems crazy to be mad at each other now that World War III has started, but I can't help feeling a little sore at him, and I wonder if Ronnie feels sore at me, too.

Sitting with his parents just a few feet away, Ronnie shakes his head as if he's trying to fight drowsiness. Like me, he's probably afraid that something bad may happen while he's asleep.

Sparky yawns again, then lays his head down on Dad's lap. His yawn makes me want to yawn, too, but I cover my mouth and try to fight it.

"Maybe you should get some sleep, Scott," Dad says.

"I don't want to."

"I think you do. It's okay. You need to rest."

Dad slides his arms under Sparky and lifts him to the bunk above Mom's. Then he turns to me. "There's room for both of you."

I climb the bunk ladder, and when my face is level with Dad's, I whisper, "You sure you'll be all right?"

Dad smiles weakly. "Yes."

When I'm on the bunk bed with Sparky, Dad covers us with the scratchy army blanket. He kisses me on the forehead, then tells Ronnie he can use the other upper bunk if he wants and Paula can have the one below it. But Paula doesn't want to leave her dad. Ronnie climbs up to the bunk catty-corner to the one Sparky and I are on. Our eyes meet when he lies down. His mom covers him with a blanket.

The bunk has a small pillow, and I lay my head on it and close my eyes but only pretend to sleep. After a while, I open one eye a tiny bit. Dad must have covered the flashlight with something because it's dimmer in the shelter but not completely dark. The Shaws and McGoverns are sitting on the floor with their backs to the wall. Janet sits by herself.

In the shadows, Dad stands in the middle of the shelter with his ear close to the water tank and taps lightly with his knuckles. A faint, hollow echo comes from inside. Then he lowers his head and looks down . . . I think toward Mom. He kneels and disappears from view.

Quietly I inch to the edge of the bunk and look over. Dad is sitting beside Mom, holding her limp hand in one of his. His other hand covers his eyes. His shoulders tremble, and I know he's hiding tears.

sixteen

Like a prisoner, I was marched through the kitchen where Sparky and Mom had started eating dinner. Sparky stopped in mid-chew and watched as we passed. I could tell he knew where Dad and I were going.

Outside, the air was cool, the moon big and round in the dark sky.

"What am I supposed to say?" I asked.

"What do you think you should say?"

"I'm sorry?"

"And that you promise never to take anything that isn't yours again."

When Dad rang the Lewandowskis' doorbell, the door

opened so quickly that I knew Mrs. Lewandowski had been waiting for us. Behind her stood Linda and three of her four brothers and sisters, all watching curiously. Linda's and my eyes met, and I felt my insides twist into a knot while my face grew hot with shame and remorse.

I apologized to Linda's mother and promised I would never take anything that wasn't mine again. Mrs. Lewandowski said she appreciated it. Then she and Dad nodded at each other as if they'd completed a deal, and my eyes met Linda's for a second time. When she looked away, I knew I was doomed.

As Dad and I walked home through the dark, I couldn't help thinking that even though all my hopes and dreams regarding Linda had been dashed, apologizing wasn't as horrible as I'd imagined it would be.

"That wasn't so bad, was it?" Dad asked.

I almost agreed but then caught myself. If I sounded too happy about apologizing, he might think it wasn't punishment enough and decide to spank me anyway. So I tried to sound unhappy. "It wasn't great. How come you didn't just spank me?"

"Don't you think you're a little too old to get spanked?"

His answer caught me by surprise. I'd never realized there was an age limit for spankings. This was the best news I'd heard in a long time.

Back home, Sparky was taking a bath. While Mom

served Dad and me a slightly cold dinner, she asked how it had gone and Dad said fine, and then she left to make sure Sparky washed behind his ears.

My brother went to bed at eight, but I was allowed to stay up until eight thirty. A small reading lamp on my night table provided just enough light to read *MAD* magazine or its inferior imitator, *Cracked.* After I was in bed, Mom and then Dad would come in and kiss me good night.

That night when Dad came in, I whispered, "What'll happen if the Russians drop the bomb?"

He thought for a moment, and the wrinkles near his eyes deepened. "It'll be the end, I'm afraid."

"Of everything?"

He seemed to hesitate, then nodded. It made me wonder if he thought that since I was now old enough not to be spanked, I was also old enough to hear the truth.

"We'll all be killed?" I asked.

"Well, some people are building bomb shelters. They say that if you can stay belowground and away from the radiation for two weeks, you can probably survive."

"Should we have one?" I asked.

"I've been thinking about it."

It seemed odd that he'd only be "thinking" when it could save our lives.

As if Dad could read my mind, he said, "They're

expensive, Scott, and a lot of people think that because we've reached the point of mutually assured destruction, war no longer makes sense." He sighed. "The problem is, wars almost never make sense — but that never stopped anyone before."

17

My eyes open and it takes a moment to remember where I am, but the sounds of the others breathing in their sleep quickly reminds me. I yawn and stretch, then become aware of dampness around my middle — and the unmistakable smell of urine. My body goes rigid. I've wet the bed, something I haven't done in years. And not only that, but I've done it in front of Ronnie and Paula...

Forget about perishing in a nuclear war; I could die from shame right now — unless I can keep it a secret. If I can somehow get Dad's attention without the others noticing, maybe he can help me figure a way out of this mess. I inch toward the edge of the bunk and look over in the dim light, where my eyes immediately meet Mr. McGovern's. He's sitting against the wall with Paula's head on his thigh while she sleeps. Against the other wall, Mr. and Mrs. Shaw lean into each other with their eyes closed. Janet sits with her head tilted down, her chin on her chest. Dad's directly below me, his head also tilted down. Lying on her back on her bunk, Mom doesn't look like she's moved at all. I inch away from the edge until I feel Sparky behind me.

Wait . . . I touch the front of my pajamas. They're dry. *It was Sparky, not me!* I feel a moment of relief, but then turmoil returns. How can I let the others know it wasn't me without humiliating him?

There's nothing to do except wait for Dad to wake up, but it's chilly on the wet mattress. I curl up for warmth and still shiver. Meanwhile, unwanted thoughts invade my mind: What will happen to us without water? The grown-ups will probably decide that one of them will go out and look for it, even though it may mean getting radiation sickness. What if the water they find is full of radiation and makes us sick, too?

Or what if we find water and stay down here for two weeks, and when we get out, we're the only ones left around here? Dad said we'd have to rebuild. But how could just the nine of us — ten if Mom gets better — do that? We'd need a lot more people.

What if Dad wasn't only talking about rebuilding things like houses and roads, but the human race as well? If Mom gets better, she could have some more babies. And so could Mrs. Shaw. And Janet, who is pretty and slim and a little younger than both Mom and Mrs. Shaw, so maybe she could have a bunch. But that still wouldn't be very many. Could Paula have babies? Maybe not right away, but soon? Like in a couple of years?

Then it hits me. If Paula is going to have babies someday, it's going to have to be with Ronnie or me.

How's *that* going to work? I don't feel like I'm ready to have babies with anyone, but Ronnie probably can't wait. If it was up to him, he'd probably want to start before we even get out of the shelter. There's no doubt in my mind that when it's time for Paula to have babies, Ronnie will be the father. He's stronger and a better athlete and better-looking. I won't stand a chance, which is kind of okay because I never really cared that much for Paula anyway.

But once Ronnie and Paula start having babies, there'll be no one left for me.

I hear a rustle below and peek over the edge. Dad's leaning over Mom's bunk, but I can't see what he's doing.

After a while, he stands up to check on Sparky and me. Our eyes meet and his nose wrinkles. I point at Sparky. Dad nods and then he's still for a moment. His eyes slide away toward the water tank. Is he thinking that if there's no water to drink, then there's none for washing pee-soaked pajamas?

eighteen

Early in July, big sheets of blueprints appeared on our dining-room table. A few days later, Sparky and I followed Dad around the backyard with two men who hammered short wooden stakes into the grass and tied a string that outlined the rectangular boundary where the new addition to our house would go—a new playroom and a bedroom for me.

The next morning, three men with pickaxes, shovels, and a wheelbarrow began digging inside the staked-off area.

By the afternoon, the hole was knee-deep and the size of big kiddie pool. Sparky and I stood on the other side of the string and watched; the men, who were Negroes and wore overalls, stole glances at us. Overalls were not an item of clothing that hung in my father's closet nor, I was pretty certain, in the closets of any of my friends' fathers. Under the overalls the men wore dingy T-shirts with small holes and tears in them.

Each man had his own way of digging. The tall, wiry one with long, sinewy arms slammed the heel of his boot against the top of the shovel to drive the blade down into the soil. Then he would arch back and use his whole body to leverage the dirt into the wheelbarrow. The paunchy man with thick undefined arms would lean against the shovel and wiggle the blade back and forth into the dirt. Then he would jam the handle against his hip and, without moving his feet, swivel toward the wheelbarrow. The third man had broad shoulders that narrowed down to his waist, and muscular arms. He looked like a dark version of the muscle builders in the magazines Dad sometimes read and was strong enough to thrust his shovel straight into the dirt, then bend his knees and toss shovelfuls into the wheelbarrow. Hardly any dirt missed.

Within a few days, the men had dug as deep as their thighs, and the rectangular hole reached to the string on all three sides. Beneath the dark brown topsoil was a layer of lighter soil mixed with sand, and below that appeared to be grayish clay. They used the pickaxes now as well as shovels, and the work went more slowly as they heaved shovelfuls of dirt and clay up onto a canvas tarp at the rim of the hole. It seemed strange that they would be digging so deep for rooms that were supposed to be above the ground.

"Maybe it's an indoor swimming pool," Sparky said.

Could *that* be it? Were they not only building an addition but a surprise swimming pool as well? Having our own pool would be a thousand times better than the pool at the country club. Not only because we'd be able to swim anytime we wanted but because we could have just our friends over instead of sharing with everyone. We could float on rafts, which weren't allowed at the club pool, and private pools had lights, so we could even swim at night.

But the best thing about having our own pool would be doing all the cannonballs we wanted! My friends and I had spent a considerable amount of time the previous summer perfecting cannonballs off the diving board at the club pool. The perfect cannonball resulted in a spout-like splash of water that rocketed straight upward from the point of entry, sometimes even splashing against the bottom of the diving board. Unfortunately, sometimes our splashes veered off at an angle and sprayed the ladies who sunned on the lounges. When that happened, they'd complain to the lifeguards and cannonballs would be banned for the rest of the day.

Seeking confirmation, Sparky and I raced into the

house, where we found Mom sitting at the kitchen table, smoking a cigarette. That was strange. Usually she only smoked on weekend nights when she and Dad had people over for dinner. And when she sat at the kitchen table, she always read a magazine. But it was the middle of the afternoon, there was no magazine, and her gaze slanted up and away into the smoky air.

"Are we getting an indoor swimming pool?" Sparky asked.

Mom scowled and crushed the cigarette out in the ashtray. "What makes you think that?"

"The hole they're digging."

"Your father didn't tell you? It's a bomb shelter."

"What's that?" asked Sparky.

"A place where we can hide in case the Commies drop the H-bomb on us," I said.

"Why?" Sparky was filled with disappointment.

"You'll have to ask your father," Mom said.

Drained of excitement, Sparky and I wandered into the den to wait for Dad to come home from work. The den had a white shag carpet, a white L-shaped couch, and walls covered with whitewashed knotty pine. Dad had made some of the furniture himself using the big DeWalt table saw in the garage. Sparky and I lay down on the carpet. White shag provided excellent ground cover for the wars I staged with my plastic army men, who, hidden in the long white strands, could sneak to within inches of each other before opening fire. The one absolute rule was no eating in the den. Once crumbs got into the shag, they were gone for good unless you went through the long white fibers with a magnifying glass and tweezers. Getting caught eating in the den was almost an automatic spanking.

"Maybe we can get Dad to change his mind," Sparky said.

"Maybe," I said, although I had my doubts. I'd learned a little about nuclear war from duck-and-cover air-raid drills at school, but most of what I knew about the Russians came from the *Rocky and Bullwinkle Show* on TV. Rocky the flying squirrel and his pal Bullwinkle J. Moose were often called upon to foil the sinister plots of Boris Badenov and his girlfriend, Natasha Fatale, who had foreign accents and were no-good spies from a no-good country clearly like Russia.

Americans were a good, peace-loving people. We had a handsome president with a pretty wife, and we wanted to live freely and play baseball and enjoy life. Russia had an ugly leader who most likely wasn't even married and only wanted to destroy America. The Russian people lived in fear of their leaders and probably weren't allowed to play sports.

So it would be too bad if we weren't getting a swimming pool, but maybe a bomb shelter wasn't such a bad thing, either.

19

Sparky and I have no dry clothes to change into, so we sit naked on the lower bunk with a blanket around our shoulders. I feel proud of my little brother for not making a fuss about wetting himself. After a while everyone is awake again, and Dad cranks the ventilator to get more fresh air in the shelter. Janet sits on the edge of Mom's bunk and feels her pulse. People stretch and move around. They glance at Mom and at Sparky and me pressed close together, but no one says anything. Paula wrinkles her nose like she can smell what Sparky did, but then whispers to her father, who speaks in a hushed tone to Dad. They may be whispering for Paula's sake, but everyone knows what they're talking about. Dad gestures at a bucket with a toilet seat on top of it.

"Won't it fill up quickly?" Mrs. Shaw asks.

Dad points at the big metal garbage can next to the toilet bucket. "It goes in here."

Paula starts to cry again. Mr. McGovern hugs her. "It's okay, honey. Everyone's going to have to use it sooner or later."

With her legs squeezed together, Paula leans against him and sobs. I feel bad for her. Maybe everyone will have to use the toilet bucket, but I wouldn't want to be the first, either.

"For Pete's sake," Mrs. Shaw grumbles. I watch in amazement as she pulls up her robe and sits down on the toilet seat. "Don't look," she says, annoyed.

I quickly turn away and hear the hard rattle as her pee strikes the bottom of the empty bucket. Soon it becomes a dribble and then stops. Mrs. Shaw focuses on Dad. "Toilet paper?"

Dad goes to a shelf and gets a roll. "I only stocked enough for four people."

"How could I forget?" Mrs. Shaw snorts. The soft sound of tissue tearing is followed by the rustle of clothes. Then in a gentle voice she says to Paula, "Okay, honey, it's your turn."

Paula sniffs.

"Go on," her father says softly.

"Noooo," Paula wails, as if she's in agony. You can't help feeling bad for her. Dad starts to crank the ventilator again. Only this time it's for the noise.

"Come on, honey," Mrs. Shaw says. "I'll make sure they don't look."

Ronnie glances at me and smirks. But he's being a jerk. Mrs. Shaw stands in front of Paula, and the rest of us look away. When Paula's finished, she comes out from behind Mrs. Shaw with her head bowed and goes back to her dad, eyes downcast.

"Anyone else?" Mrs. Shaw asks. I have to go and now that some of the others have, I figure what's the big deal and maybe it will make Paula feel better. So I say me.

"Well, aren't you the brave one?" Mrs. Shaw says, and I'm not sure whether she means it or is being sarcastic. Since all Sparky and I have to cover us is the blanket, he has to get up with me. Like a four-legged creature, we shuffle over to the toilet bucket. Once again Mrs. Shaw blocks the view and Dad cranks the ventilator. I really do have to go, but I can't with Sparky standing next to me and all these people around. It's as if everything down there is blocked, and in an instant I go from the proud feeling of being brave to feeling completely embarrassed, because even with the ventilator going, the others will be able to tell that nothing is happening. That's when Mrs. Shaw whispers, "Think about waterfalls and garden hoses."

The next thing I know, pee splashes into the bucket, where it mixes with Paula's and Mrs. Shaw's, and I wonder why it was so hard to go before.

Janet goes next, and then one by one, the fathers pee in the bucket, only Dad doesn't crank the ventilator for them. After a while, the only one who hasn't gone is Ronnie. I glance at him, but instead of a smirk, his face is scrunched up as if he's in agony.

Mr. Shaw squeezes his arm. "You better go."

"Shut up," he grunts.

A jolt jumps through me like an electric charge. I've never heard a kid say that to a parent or any grown-up. I wait for Mr. or Mrs. Shaw to scold him, but there's only silence until Ronnie lets out a low moan as if his bladder is about to explode.

A moment later, when I hear a gurgle, I assume Ronnie is going in his pajamas. But Dad quickly looks up at the water tank, and his eyebrows practically leap off his head. It's the sound of running water!

Maybe it's the relief of knowing we have water or the sound of it sloshing through the pipes, but Ronnie races to the toilet bucket and goes.

twenty

When Dad came home from work, Sparky and I followed him into his and Mom's bedroom, where he took off his suit, shirt, and tie, removed his brown leather shoes and placed shoe trees in them. Then he unsnapped the elastic garters around his calves that held up his long, thin socks, and put on dungarees, a gray Fruit of the Loom sweatshirt, white wool socks, and old tennis sneakers.

"Are we getting a bomb shelter?" I asked.

"I'll tell you at dinner," he said, and headed outside. In the summer, Dad often did yard work before dinner. Sparky and I followed him into the backyard, where he stopped to look at the hole.

"How deep will it get?" I asked.

"Pretty deep," Dad said.

"Sure would make a good pool," said Sparky.

"Yes, it would," said Dad.

"A pool would be fun," Sparky said.

"We need a shelter more than we need a pool."

"Couldn't it be a shelter *and* a pool?" Sparky asked.

Just then, Mom called us in. During dinner, Dad told Sparky how there was a chance we might go to war with the Russians.

"Why don't they like us?" my brother asked. "Did we do something bad to them?"

"They don't agree with our form of government."

"What's that?"

Dad tried to explain, but it was hard to go from what a democracy was to why the Russians would want to blow us to smithereens.

"If the Russians win, will we be their prisoners?" I asked.

"Not necessarily," Dad said. "A lot of people think that if there's a war, neither side can win." He must have seen the confused expressions on our faces, because he added, "Both sides have so many bombs that there's a good chance we'll destroy so much of each other's countries that no one will be able to claim victory."

That didn't make sense. Why would anyone go to war if they knew ahead of time that neither side could win? Thus far in the conversation, Mom had remained quiet. Now she slowly shook her head. "Mutually assured destruction. It's ridiculous."

Dad leveled his gaze at her. "I agree, but it's a possibility."

"Don't scare them," Mom said, a bit harshly. The "them" she was referring to was Sparky and me.

"They asked why we're building a shelter—" Dad began to reply.

"Not a shelter, a *bomb* shelter," Mom interjected. "And *we're* not building it—*you* are."

They stared at each other. Then Mom got up and hurried out of the room. Dad let out a sigh. "Finish your dinner, boys." He left to go find Mom.

21

As water races through the pipes and into the tank, I hear someone's throat catch and see Mrs. Shaw hug her husband with relief.

"There was probably an obstruction in the line," says Mr. McGovern. "The water pressure must have forced it loose."

Dad takes a glass from a shelf and fills it, then sniffs tentatively before taking a sip. He grimaces.

"What's wrong?" Mr. Shaw asks. Dad hands him the glass, and Ronnie's dad tries a little, then spits it at the drain in the middle of the floor and wipes his mouth. "*Achh!* It's awful."

"You didn't rinse the system when it was installed?" Mr. McGovern's question sounds critical.

Dad doesn't answer.

"Is that bad?" Mrs. Shaw asks with alarm, directing the question to Mr. McGovern. "Will it hurt us?"

Mr. McGovern pauses thoughtfully. "I don't think so. It won't taste good, but we won't have to drink it forever."

Mrs. Shaw takes the glass from her husband and sips. Her face goes hard. "Well, at least we can wash our hands."

Dad gazes up at the water tank. "Maybe we shouldn't. I'm worried about using it for anything except drinking."

"You don't think there'll be more if this runs out?" Mr. Shaw asks.

Dad shrugs. "I don't know."

"Actually," Mr. McGovern begins, then pauses as if he wants to make sure everyone is listening. "Given the circumstances, I suspect we'll have all the water we'll need."

This comment is met with silence. The grown-ups share the kind of meaningful look that makes kids nervous.

"Why?" Paula looks anxiously at her father, who lets out a reluctant sigh like he doesn't want to give the answer.

But he does. "Because, honey, there probably isn't anyone else left to use it."

Paula begins to sob again.

Dad pours just enough water into a bowl so that we can wash our hands. Then he uses a corner of a towel to gently wipe Mom's face. Sparky and I huddle under the blanket. The sour odor of urine from our wet pajamas mixes with the damp mildew smell of the shelter. I would ask Dad if he'd wash our pajamas, but I know what his answer will be.

He does make a pitcher of Tang. There are only four glasses, so each family shares and Janet gets one for herself. Even with the Tang, the bitter metallic taste from the pipes comes through. By now everyone's a little hungry, and we eat Spam on the bread and broken crackers Mom brought from the kitchen. The Spam tastes spicy and salty, and everyone drinks more Tang. But Dad's being careful. Whether on crackers or bread, we each have about half a sandwich's worth of food and maybe a cupful to drink.

"Herb thinks the water won't be a problem," Mrs. Shaw reminds Dad.

Sitting beside Mom, Dad says, "I don't know how anyone could be certain."

Mr. McGovern exhales noisily, as if he's dealing with

an idiot. "It's a gravity-fed system, Richard. It doesn't depend on electricity or any other kind of power."

"Willing to bet your life on that?" Dad asks sharply, as if he's getting annoyed with Mr. McGovern's attitude. Mr. McGovern exchanges a look with Mr. and Mrs. Shaw, but no one says anything more.

Sparky wriggles under the scratchy blanket. "What about our pajamas?"

Dad shakes his head. "I don't think so, Edward. They won't dry down here, and this could be all the water we'll get."

"Please, Dad?" Sparky whines.

"I said no."

"If they put them back on, won't their body heat eventually dry them?" Mr. Shaw asks.

"Want to try it, boys?" Dad asks us.

Even though Sparky and I are both squirmy and itchy and constantly tugging little bits of blanket from each other, I'd rather be huddling naked with him than put my damp, pee-stinky pajamas back on.

We've eaten and gone to the bathroom, and now there's nothing else to do except sit. Ronnie catches my eye and I know that he wants to talk, but I still don't know how I feel. He may be my best friend, but my scraped elbows and throbbing knee are a reminder of last night's fight. All he's ever done is get me in trouble and make me think about things I don't want to think about. Maybe it's good that I'm sharing the blanket with Sparky, because that means I can't go talk to him.

Dad tries the radio, and again there's nothing but silence and static.

"Did you test it?" Mrs. Shaw asks. "I mean, before?"

Dad doesn't answer, which is kind of an answer in itself. Mrs. Shaw lets out a loud, dramatic sigh of disapproval.

twenty-two

It wasn't long before the hole in the backyard came up to the Negro men's chests. Now two men shoveled, filling a metal bucket, which the third hoisted out of the hole and dumped into the wheelbarrow. The men also began to encounter large rocks, some the size of basketballs, that had to be pried out of the ground and heaved onto the grass beside the hole.

The men always arrived early in the morning and usually stayed until around five o'clock, when a pickup truck would come get them. There wasn't room for all three in the truck cab, so one would sit in front and two would climb into the back. The man who drove the pickup was white.

Each day the men brought metal lunch boxes and thermoses. By now they were used to me and Sparky watching and would sometimes nod at us. And sometimes they would carry on a conversation as if we weren't there.

One day when the sun was like a yellow oven in the sky, sweat dripped from the men's faces. The collars of their T-shirts were dark with moisture, and the skin on their bare arms glistened. They paused often, dabbing the sweat with bandannas and shielding their eyes. I watched the muscular man climb out of the hole and unscrew the cap on his thermos. Only a drop or two came out. The other two leaned on their shovels as if they needed the support. Tracks of sweat lined their faces.

I went into the house. It was hot in the kitchen, and Mom was sitting at the table with a tall glass of iced tea streaked with condensation. She dabbed her forehead with one of Dad's white handkerchiefs.

I gestured to the glass. "I think the men outside could use some."

Mom got up and took three glasses from the kitchen cabinet. "Get some ice."

I took an ice tray from the freezer. Hating the way the frosty metal stuck to my fingertips, I quickly placed the tray in the sink and ran water over it, then pulled the metal lever to crack the ice so Mom could get the pieces out. A few moments later, I carried the glasses outside on a platter.

It was hard to tell whether the men's grins reflected more delight or surprise.

"What's your name, son?" asked the paunchy one.

"Scott," I said.

"Well, Scott, much obliged."

In no time, the glasses were empty. Back in the kitchen, Mom raised her eyebrows. "They asked for more?"

"No, but I think they'll need it."

Mom glanced outside, squinting at the brightness. "That's very thoughtful of you, sweetheart." She started toward the refrigerator, then paused to wipe something out of the corner of her eye.

"You okay?" I asked.

"Yes, Scott." She took out the pitcher of iced tea and put it on the platter, then left the kitchen without another word.

23

After a while, Dad unfolds the card table and invites the others to sit. There are four chairs, and Mr. and Mrs. Shaw and Mr. McGovern sit in three of them. Paula sits on her father's lap. Dad returns to Mom's side.

"You sit with them," Janet says to him. "I'll stay with Mrs. Porter."

Dad hesitates, then gets up, letting Janet take his place. At the table, the grown-ups sit silently in the dim light. Sparky picks at the lint on the scratchy army blanket we're huddled under. Ronnie gnaws at his fingernails.

"You kids want to play a game?" Dad asks.

Paula shakes her head. Ronnie gives me a questioning look. I'm still uncertain about whether to be angry about the fight, and somehow it feels wrong to play games when everything is so serious. But there's nothing else to do, so I lean toward the shelf to get the checkerboard.

"Hey!" Sparky yelps when I accidentally pull some blanket away from him, leaving parts of his naked body exposed to the cool air and others' eyes. He yanks the blanket back, and the next thing I know, I'm completely naked.

By the time my eyes go to Paula, she's looking away, but I have a feeling that's not where she was looking an instant ago. Ronnie grins his jerky grin, which makes me mad at him all over again. I grab the blanket and manage to cover myself, but Sparky grabs it back, and soon we're in a tug-of-war.

"Stop it!" Dad orders, getting up. "I've got an idea."

He holds my damp pajamas under the ventilator while Mr. McGovern turns the crank and blows air on them. After a while, Paula's dad stops to rest, and Mr. Shaw takes over. After two cranks, he's frowning. You can see that it's harder than he expected. His eyes go to his wife.

"Do you have to keep doing that?" Mrs. Shaw asks. "It's cold enough in here."

Dad backs away from the ventilator and hands the pajamas to me. They're cold and still damp.

"Sit on them," Mr. McGovern suggests. "They'll get warmer."

I do what he says, and it's not long before the

pajamas stop feeling cold under my butt. While Paula looks away, I pull on the top and then the bottoms. They're still damp in spots, and when Sparky leans close and sniffs, he wrinkles his nose. But at least now I can get out from under the blanket.

Meanwhile, Ronnie's looking at the checkerboard. Our eyes meet, but I'm still mad at him for grinning when Sparky pulled the blanket off me. If our parents weren't here, I'd tell him he'd have to apologize before I'd play with him. Only knowing Ronnie, he never would.

Sparky and I thumb wrestle. To keep it interesting, I let him win a couple of times, but it gets boring just the same. He's still wrapped in the blanket. I doubt he'd wear his pajamas even if Dad dried them. He's much pickier about things like that than I am. After a while, he says, "Dad, I'm hungry."

"We're all hungry, Edward."

"But, Dad . . . " he whines.

"Let him have something," Mrs. Shaw says.

"There won't be enough food to—" Dad begins, but Mrs. Shaw cuts him short.

"He's a child and he's scared. Food comforts them. We'll worry about running out later."

Dad sighs as if he disagrees but has decided not to argue. It feels strange to hear Mrs. Shaw talk about comfort food, since whenever I ate at their house, she made TV dinners.

While Dad starts to open another can of Spam, Ronnie and Paula share a look. They're also hungry. But I know that they won't say anything because it's our bomb shelter and our food. So it's up to me: "Us, too, Dad."

Ronnie gives me a nod as if he appreciates it, but I look away.

"How long before we've eaten everything?" Mr. McGovern asks.

Dad gestures to the shelf. "That's all we've got."

On the shelf are about two dozen cans of Spam, tuna fish, sardines, some small jars of peanut butter and jelly, bread, and crackers. Even I can see that if we only have one more meal today, and only two small meals for every day to come, it won't last long.

We devour the extra Spam and Tang that Dad gives us. Sparky yawns. "What time is it?"

We don't know. No one was wearing a watch when we were awakened in the middle of the night by the sirens.

"I wonder if it's even noon," says Mr. McGovern.

Everyone is quiet. Are they thinking what I'm thinking? That it feels hopeless? Not even a day has passed, and I'm already bored, dirty, hungry, and smelly in my pee-stinky pajamas. How are we ever going to stay down here for two weeks?

twenty-four

One Saturday just before lunchtime, Sparky came in and asked why the Shaws were in our backyard.

Dad, who'd just come home from tennis and was still wearing his white shorts and shirt, went outside. Mom, Sparky, and I followed. Ronnie's parents were standing beside the hole with their collie, Leader. This was surprising, because even though they only lived one house away and always said hello and acted friendly, my parents and the Shaws never went out together or had dinner with us kids the way we did with other families.

We stood on one side of the hole, and the Shaws stood on the other. Ronnie's parents smiled like they thought something was funny. "That's quite a hole," said Mr. Shaw.

Dad didn't answer.

"What's next?" asked Mr. Shaw.

"Sorry?" Dad said.

Ronnie's dad pointed. "Something's going in there, isn't it?"

"Yes, and over it will go Scott's new bedroom and a playroom," Dad said.

"So what's going in there?" Mr. Shaw asked.

"A shelter," Dad said.

"A bomb shelter," Mom added, annoyed, as if it was silly to pretend it was anything else.

Everyone was quiet, then Mr. Shaw said, "Well, good luck." He and Mrs. Shaw and Leader left.

Back in the house, Dad went to change out of his tennis clothes while Sparky and I set the kitchen table for lunch.

"How come the Shaws wanted to see the hole?" I asked.

"I guess they were curious," Mom answered.

"They never came over before," I said.

"We never had a hole before," Sparky said, as if it was obvious.

Mom laughed.

But when Dad came in, she stopped smiling. Usually at meals our parents would talk or ask us questions about our plans for the day. But that day Mom and Dad were quiet. Sparky kept shooting me puzzled looks, and I'd shrug.

Finally Mom said, "You knew that was going to happen sooner or later."

Dad took a bite of tuna-fish sandwich and gave her the "not in front of the kids" look.

"Don't you think they should know?" Mom asked. "They're part of this, too." She turned to us. "Your friends may say something about the bomb shelter."

"Like what?" I asked.

"They may want to know why we're building it."

"Because of the Russians, right?" I said.

Dad nodded.

"The problem is that not everyone agrees with what we're doing," Mom said.

"Why not?" asked Sparky.

Mom looked at Dad as if it was his job to answer.

"People have different ideas about whether we'll go to war or not," Dad said. "Some think it's likely, and some don't."

"You think it's likely, right?" I asked.

"Well . . . " Dad paused. "I think it's possible."

"And the bomb shelter is for just in case," Sparky said. "Like a spare tire."

"Right," said Dad.

It got quiet again.

"So . . . what's the problem?" I asked.

Mom and Dad looked at each other. I expected Dad to answer, since he was sort of in charge of the bomb shelter. But it was Mom who said, "The problem is that everyone knows about it."

"The threat of war?" I said, confused.

"No, the bomb shelter." Mom looked at me questioningly. "Do you know anyone else who has one?"

"No."

"Your mom's worried that other kids may make fun of you," Dad said.

Sparky made a fist. "Anyone makes fun of me, I'll punch 'em in the face."

"Why would they make fun of us?" I asked.

"Some people think it's silly," Mom said. "They don't believe there'll be a war. And there are other people who think it's silly because if there is a war and everything's destroyed, what would be the point of living?"

"Everyone wants to live," I said.

"Even if there was nothing left?" Mom asked. "No electricity. No jobs. Hardly any food."

"We'd rebuild," Dad said. "Think about what it must have been like when the Pilgrims first got here."

"What a wonderful existence they had," Mom muttered sourly.

"They had Thanksgiving," Sparky said. "After the war, we could have Thanksgiving, too."

Mom's eyes suddenly filled with tears. Her chair scraped loudly as she pushed it back and hurried out of the kitchen.

Dad stared at the empty doorway, then let out a sigh and got up. "Sorry, boys. This is something your mom and I disagree about."

He left Sparky and me at the table. Our parents' voices came down the hall from their bedroom, too faint to make out what they were saying. But we could hear the tone. Mom was upset and angry, and Dad was trying to get her to calm down.

Back in the kitchen, Sparky whispered, "What's so bad about Thanksgiving?"

25

Ronnie catches me looking at the checkers game and raises his eyebrow. I turn away. I may be going crazy with nothing to do, but I'm still not playing with him.

"Come on, you two, let bygones be bygones," Dad says.

I bet he wouldn't say that if he knew what Ronnie said about him.

"Did something happen?" Mr. Shaw asks.

Ronnie and I share another look, neither of us willing to tell.

"They got into a scrape last night," Dad says.

"About?" asks Mr. Shaw.

"You'll have to ask them."

Ronnie's dad studies us.

"Seriously, boys, whatever it was about, how could it matter now?" Dad asks.

"You'd be surprised," I mutter.

"Shut up," Ronnie growls.

"Why don't you tell them?" I dare him.

Ronnie narrows his eyes like he'll kill me if I tell. As if he could do anything with all these grown-ups around. Suddenly it's so stupid, it almost feels funny. I stick my tongue out at him. He blinks, then grins, and sticks his tongue back at me.

Dad and Janet take turns sitting with Mom. When Dad's with her, he holds her hand. Now and then, Janet takes her pulse. I know why they're watching her, but I can't say anything because I don't want to scare Sparky. But I'm scared. I don't want her to die. And what will happen if she does, and we still have to stay down here for two weeks? The idea is so awful, I have to make myself think of other things.

Now that we've stuck our tongues out at each other, it feels dumb to stay angry, so Ronnie and I play checkers. Sparky watches and goes "uh-huh" when he thinks I've made a good move and "nuh-uh" when he doesn't. Normally I'd tell him to get lost, but that would leave him with nothing to do.

The grown-ups start to play cards. I guess they need to find a way to pass the time, too. It's weird because no one knows what time it really is. Is it daytime up there? Night?

Do day and night still exist?

"Two weeks of this?" Mrs. Shaw mutters to no one in particular.

Minutes, hours, countless games of cards and checkers have passed. Sparky wants to take a nap, so Dad puts a towel over the wet spot and helps him up into our bunk. Mr. Shaw lies on some blankets on the floor, and Ronnie squeezes beside his mom on a bunk, just as Paula does with her father. Janet starts to lean her head against the concrete wall, so Dad makes a small bed out of pillows for her on the floor then turns to me.

"You want to sleep?"

I shake my head. Dad and I sit at the card table. My fingers scratch at the red plastic surface, and I can't help thinking about school and my teacher, Mr. Kasman, and, once again, about my friends. . . . I feel a deep sadness like nothing I've ever felt before. Why Can't You Be Like Johnny? . . . Freak O' Nature . . . Linda . . . Can they all be gone? I know what the answer probably is, but it's so hard to believe.

Mr. Shaw starts to snore. The others breathe deeply and steadily. Opposite me, Dad stares at his interlaced fingers.

I whisper, "Do you think it killed everybody up there?"

There's down here and up there. The ones who feel like they're buried are alive, while the ones who aren't buried probably aren't alive. Everything's upside down. Dad gazes at me with sad eyes. "There must have been other people with shelters. People who were less obvious about it." He sounds like he wishes he'd been less obvious, too.

"But they would have dug a hole, right?" I know for certain that Freak O' Nature's and Why Can't You Be Like Johnny?'s and Linda's parents didn't dig holes for bomb shelters, and I have a feeling that if anyone else we knew had, we would have heard about it. It's not fair. Freak O' Nature and Why Can't You Be Like Johnny? never did mean things to anyone and never even *met* a Russian. . . .

My thoughts are interrupted by faint grinding sounds coming from Sparky's direction. He's lying on the bunk, eyes closed as if he's asleep, but his jaw works back and forth.

"Edward?" Dad whispers.

My brother doesn't respond. He's doing it in his sleep.

"He ever do that before?" Dad asks.

I shake my head. Dad watches him for a moment, then glances at Mom.

"She's not going to be okay, is she?" I ask.

With his elbows on the table, Dad brings his clasped hands to his forehead like he's praying. "I don't know, Scott."

But deep down, I think he does.

A slight rustling wakes me. Dad and I have fallen asleep at the table with our heads on our arms. Out of the corner of my eye, I watch Sparky quietly creep down from the bunk. I'd ask him where he's going, but I don't want to wake everyone.

Naked, he heads toward the toilet bucket, so I assume he just has to go. Still sleepy, my heavy eyelids are starting to close when I hear the metallic clink of the big refuse can. Sparky tips open the top and throws his dirty pajamas in.

"Mr. Porter? Mr. Porter!" Janet is sitting up, staring at Mom, who is still lying on her back on the bunk. My first thought is that the worst has happened, but then I see that her eyes are open.

"Don't look." Dad gets up quickly.

"Why not?" I ask.

"Because—" He stops. When Mom hears his voice, her eyes move toward him.

"Gwen?" Dad sounds hopeful and excited.

Her eyes stay on him, but she doesn't move.

The others wake and look. Dad kneels beside Mom. "Gwen?"

No answer.

"What is it?" Mrs. Shaw whispers.

"She's awake." Dad tenderly strokes Mom's cheek. "Can you hear me, sweetheart?"

But Mom's expression remains blank.

The others slowly climb out of the bunks and gather around. Mom's eyes move as she looks at them, but there's no sign of recognition.

"Gwen?" Dad says again.

Her eyes go back to him.

"Gwen, nod if you can hear me."

Mom still doesn't react.

Dad holds a finger up in front of her face and moves it slowly left. Her eyes follow it, but when Dad moves his finger back, her gaze remains directed at the wall.

"Gwen? Honey?" he says again, anxiously.

Her eyes slowly come back to him. But her face is blank. Dad picks up her hand and squeezes it. It looks limp in his. "Sweetheart?" His voice is full of uncertainty.

She doesn't respond. Dad puts her hand down, then turns away and hides his face.

twenty-six

When school began that fall, we had a new teacher and new desks. The teacher was skinny, with hollowed cheeks and a dark shadow over his jaw. He wore a gray suit that looked too big, a thin black tie, and a white shirt. Except for gym, it was the first time we'd ever had a man teacher.

"Welcome to sixth grade," he said. "My name is Mr. Kasman, and we have something in common. This is a new grade for you and a new school for me. If you look inside your desk, you will find a strip of oaktag. Please write your first name in large neat letters and place it on your desk where I can see it."

Our new desks didn't have hinged tops like the old ones. To get things from inside, we had to bend down and squint into them or feel around blindly with our hands. We'd all begun to work on our name cards when the classroom's public-address speaker crackled on: "Hello, students, and welcome back to Willis Road for another exciting year of learning." It was Principal Sharp. "A lot has changed over the summer. We have some new teachers, a new soundproof ceiling, and, as you've probably already noticed, new desks with scratch-proof desktops. After what happened last year, I'm sure you know why we got them. I hope you all have a great first day."

The PA went silent. "What happened last year?" Mr. Kasman asked.

Paula raised her hand.

"Yes, uh . . . " Mr. Kasman squinted at her name card. "Paula?"

"The boys carved things into the desks. Then they couldn't write on them because their pens went through the paper."

Mr. Kasman ran his fingers over the shiny hard surface of a desk in the front row. Then he said, "Please finish your name cards."

I went back to work, but a scratching sound started behind me. With his left arm resting on his desk, Puddin' Belly Wright appeared to be hunched forward, gazing toward the front of the room. But behind his left arm, his right hand was clenched around a bent paper clip, busy scratching at the surface of his new scratch-proof desk.

Puddin' Belly was a big, strong, chubby kid who lived a block away from us and often came around to play fungo baseball and touch football. His real name was Stuart Wright, but his belly bounced and jiggled when he ran, and somehow he'd acquired that nickname. Puddin' Belly would do almost anything if dared, or if even just asked. One morning a few days later, while Mr. Kasman wrote on the blackboard, Ronnie slid him a note. Puddin' Belly read it and raised his hand. "Hey, Mr. Kasman, how come you became a teacher?"

"I'm not a horse," Mr. Kasman said, without pausing from what he was writing.

"Huh?"

"You said 'hey,' and he said he's not a horse," Paula explained.

"Huh?" Puddin' Belly said again.

"Forget it." Mr. Kasman turned from the board. "I became a teacher because I think it's an important job."

"All of the teachers in this school are ladies," said Puddin' Belly. "Except for Mr. Brown, the gym teacher."

"Are you implying that the only teaching job a man should have is gym?" asked Mr. Kasman.

Puddin' Belly wasn't implying anything. He was simply repeating what Ronnie had told him to say. Now that the subject had been broached without Mr. Kasman getting mad, Ronnie must have felt safe to add his two cents. "I think what Stuart means is that men usually don't become teachers."

"My father teaches economics at Hofstra," said Paula.

"That's college," said Ronnie.

"Mr. Kasman?" the PA squawked. It was one of the secretaries. "Can you come down to the office for a moment?"

"Take out your grammar workbooks, and work on pages fourteen and fifteen," Mr. Kasman said, and left.

Ronnie went to the back of the room to sharpen his pencil. The grinding filled our ears. When it stopped, he didn't return to his desk. Instead, he looked up at the new sound-absorbing white cork squares in the ceiling. Holding the pencil at the point, he flicked his wrist. The pencil flew up and stuck, hanging from the ceiling like a thin yellow stalactite.

Ronnie went to the front of the room, took a new pencil from the box on Mr. Kasman's desk, and sharpened it. This time the whole room watched. A moment later, there were two yellow stalactites in the ceiling.

Puddin' Belly flipped his pencil at the ceiling. It bounced off and fell to the floor. Freak O' Nature flipped his pencil. Same result. Eric Flom tried it. Still the same result.

"Stand guard, Scott," Ronnie ordered.

Standing guard was tricky because you had to be in the doorway and watch without being seen by the teacher you were on the lookout for. I'd perfected a method of keeping the door ajar with my foot while sticking just enough of my face out so I could see with one eye. It was nothing any other kid couldn't do, but since I'd been the first to think of it, it had become my role.

By now there was a line of boys at the pencil sharpener and nonstop grinding. Kids asked Ronnie to demonstrate his technique. Soon more pencils were stuck in the ceiling.

Down the hall, Mr. Kasman came around the corner. I backed out of the doorway. "He's coming!"

Everyone hurried to their desks and got to work in their grammar workbooks.

Mr. Kasman came in and sat down and wrote something in his notebook. Then he noticed the empty pencil box.

Then he looked at us.

Then he looked up.

27

The grown-ups sit at the table and talk. The kids sit on the bunks like spectators.

"Maybe she just needs time to recover," Mrs. Shaw says.

"Anyone ever seen anything like this?" Dad asks.

"That depends on what you mean by *this*," Mr. McGovern answers. I think he's talking about his son, Paula's brother, Teddy.

"Mr. Porter?" Janet says from the bunk where she's sitting next to Mom. "She needs to be turned or she'll get bedsores."

"Now?" Dad asks.

"The sooner the better, sir."

One of Mr. McGovern's eyebrows dips. "And you know this because?"

"I was studying to be a nurse, sir."

"You? Where?" Mr. McGovern sounds a little mean.

"Long Island College Hospital of Nursing, sir."

"Never heard of it," Mr. McGovern says dismissively.

For a moment, everyone goes still. I wish I could ask Mr. McGovern why he said that. Then the moment passes, and Dad helps Janet turn Mom onto her side.

That's when we all smell it.

As if the mildew and pee odors aren't bad enough, now there's this. I feel embarrassed for Mom and try not to watch while Dad and Janet remove her soiled clothes and the sheet she was lying on. It all goes into the big refuse can. Dad relents about using water for something other than drinking. For a sponge and towels, Janet tears off the bottom part of her robe. After the rags are used, they also go into the can.

When they're finished, Mom is lying on her side with her bare bottom and legs exposed. Dad takes the sheet from the upper bunk and tears it in half. He and Janet tuck it around Mom, who is as still and quiet as before.

My stomach growls, but I know we need to ration the food, so I keep quiet. Ronnie, me, and Sparky, who's now wearing a little loincloth Janet made for him, have played about a thousand games of checkers. Dad comes over and suggests we switch to Parcheesi. He makes the slightest gesture with his head toward Paula, so I say, "Want to play, Paula?"

With his back to her so she can't see, Dad smiles and nods.

We four kids play Parcheesi, but all I think about is food. Since it's impossible to tell whether it's day or night, people climb into the bunks when they're tired, but now it's more like we take long naps rather than sleep for one extended period. Mr. McGovern snores. Sparky grinds his teeth. Mrs. Shaw talks in her sleep. Once she said, "Ronnie, stop that right now!" and another time it was, "I hate this."

But no one sleeps for long; hunger keeps waking us.

"Is it time to eat, Herr Kapitän?" Mr. McGovern asks.

Sparky looks up curiously. "What's that mean, Dad?"

"He's making a joke," Dad says.

"Well?" Mr. McGovern doesn't sound like he's making a joke.

Dad points at the remaining cans on the shelf. "I only stored enough food for four. Now we're ten. At this rate, we'll use it all up by the end of the first week."

"And you're the one who decides when we eat?" asks Mr. McGovern.

"It's my family's food," Dad points out.

"Maybe it was . . . before what happened," Mr. McGovern says. "But now that we're all in this together, shouldn't it belong to all of us?"

Dad and Mr. McGovern face each other.

"You know," Dad grumbles, "none of us would be alive right now if it wasn't for me. Did it ever occur to you to utter two very simple words like 'thank you'?"

Paula's dad glares. "Thank you, Richard. However, don't forget that if you'd had your way, the rest of us would be dead."

Dad narrows his eyes. "Yes, I tried to keep people out, but only to protect my family. It was horrible and something that's going to haunt me for a long time. But how was I supposed to know how many people were up there? What was I supposed to do? Let everyone in? How'd you like it if there were twenty people in here right now? Or thirty? You might as well be up there."

"I think I'd rather die than know I was responsible for the deaths of others," Mrs. Shaw says.

I've never seen Dad argue or fight with our neighbors before. Except for the disagreements my parents sometimes had, I'm not sure I ever saw grown-ups get cross with one another before.

Now Dad turns to Mr. Shaw. "You want to tell her or should I?"

Mr. Shaw gazes up at the ceiling and lets out a long

breath. "Steph, after I got you and Ronnie down here, I . . . " He trails off and lowers his head.

"He helped me keep the others out," Dad finishes for him. "I couldn't have done it without him."

twenty-eight

Once he'd gone around the room with a yardstick and knocked the pencils out of the ceiling, Mr. Kasman made all the boys stay in for lunch detention.

"What was the point of that?" he asked us.

No one answered.

"Ronnie?" By now Mr. Kasman had figured out who the likely ringleader was.

"It was interesting," Ronnie said.

"How?"

"Just to see if you could do it."

"It appears that most of you figured out you could do it."

"But then we had to figure out if we could keep doing it." Ronnie grinned.

"Was it worth missing recess?"

No one answered.

"Scott?"

I answered honestly. "Well, uh, just this once, yeah."

A couple of guys chuckled. Even Mr. Kasman smirked as if, deep down inside, he understood. Maybe it was good that we had a man teacher, because I had a feeling a woman teacher would never understand. "Okay, but this is the last time, right?"

"Does that mean we can go outside?" asked Ronnie.

"No, it means you'll stay here today, and if it ever happens again, you'll get a week of lunch detentions."

"So we just have to sit here?" asked Freak O' Nature. We'd never had lunch detention before.

"We can talk," said Mr. Kasman. That was strange. Most teachers didn't want to talk to us. They just wanted us to do our work and be quiet. Maybe Mr. Kasman was too new to know that yet.

Ronnie whispered something to Puddin' Belly, who raised his hand. "Are you a beatnik, Mr. Kasman?"

"What's a beatnik?" Mr. Kasman asked.

"They live in Greenwich Village and listen to jazz," said Eric Flom.

Dickie Keller raised his hand. "They play bongos and read poetry."

"And snap their fingers and say 'Cool, man, cool,' " said Freak O' Nature.

"How many of your parents listen to jazz?" Mr. Kasman asked.

A few hands went up around the room.

"Are they beatniks?" our teacher asked.

The kids who'd raised their hands shook their heads.

"Who knows what the word *stereotype* means?"

Silence. If Paula had been there, she probably would have known, but it was only us guys.

Mr. Kasman opened the dictionary. "To stereotype means 'to characterize someone, usually in a negative or unfair way. To make a generalization about them.' So saying that all beatniks listen to jazz and read poetry would be a generalization, but not necessarily in a negative way. But saying that all Russians are evil would be stereotyping them in a pejorative way." Gazing out at a small sea of blank faces he added, "*Pejorative* means negative or unfair."

"But the Russians *are* evil," said Ronnie.

"Dirty Commies," Freak O' Nature said in a low tough-guy voice.

"Why are they dirty?" Mr. Kasman asked.

"They don't believe in God," said Eric Flom. "And the Russian people are starving because the Communists spend all their money on missiles and bombs."

"They take away your freedom," said Dickie Keller.

"You can't vote and there's no freedom of speech and you'll get sent to Siberia if you say something the leaders don't like."

"Why?" asked our teacher.

Everyone went quiet.

"Well, come on," Mr. Kasman said. "Why would they do all those things?"

Dickie raised his arm halfway. "Because . . . they're evil?"

"What if they just have different beliefs?" our teacher asked. "Communism is based on the ideas of a philosopher named Karl Marx, who believed that if all people were equal and were treated equally, they would live in a state of Utopia."

Mr. Kasman must have sensed our confusion because he said, "It's not a state like Rhode Island. It's a state of mind. Marx believed that if no one has more than anyone else and no one is better than anyone else, then everyone will be equally happy."

I raised my hand. "You mean, if no one has anything, then they don't have more than anyone else?"

"In a way."

"What's so great about that?" asked Ronnie.

"Marx thought it was great. I'm not sure I do."

I raised my hand again. "If everyone's equal, who settles arguments?"

A smile grew on Mr. Kasman's lips. "That . . . is a very

good question, Scott. There would still be a ruler and a government, and the government would make those decisions."

"But then everyone wouldn't really be equal," I said.

"Right!" Mr. Kasman seemed pleased I'd figured that out.

I'd been right in class before, but I'm not sure a teacher had ever said so with as much praise. It felt good, and for the first time, I began to understand why Paula raised her hand so much.

Too bad Mom wasn't there to see it.

29

If no one moves or speaks, the loudest sound is the grumbling of our stomachs. That, along with being trapped down here, makes everyone moody and irritable.

"At least give us more to drink," Mr. Shaw says to Dad. "I'd rather have Tang in my stomach than nothing at all."

"What if we run out of water?" Dad replies.

"I told you that won't happen," says Mr. McGovern.

"And I told *you* that we can't know for sure," Dad shoots back sharply.

It seems like Paula's dad doubts almost everything my dad says. Just like he doubted Janet was going to college to learn to be a nurse. Is it because Mr. McGovern teaches college himself? The tension between Dad and the other adults is always just below the surface. When it comes out, Ronnie and I share perplexed looks. Everything is so strange. Our parents getting angry at one another. Mom lying mutely on the bunk. The sadness of Paula being here without her mom and brother.

And wondering all the while what has become of the world on the other side of the trapdoor.

"This was a mistake," Mr. Shaw mutters. "It's over. All we're doing is postponing the inevitable."

"Don't talk that way," Dad says.

"Don't tell me how to talk," Mr. Shaw snaps back.

"Steven, the children." Mrs. Shaw puts a hand on her husband's knee. I wonder if Mr. Shaw will snap at her, too, but he doesn't. What would they be saying if we kids weren't here?

There's still nothing on the radio except bent sound and static.

Mrs. Shaw smirks. "Is there something you don't want to miss, Richard?"

"We're supposed to listen to the Civil Defense channels," Dad replies. "They're supposed to tell us what to do."

"Aren't we doing what we're supposed to do?" Mrs. Shaw asks ironically.

"It *would* be nice to think that someone else has survived," Mr. McGovern adds.

"They have," Dad says. "Lots of people built shelters."

"Lots," Mrs. Shaw echoes, like she's laughing at him.

We hear a soft, low groan. Dad squats down close to Mom. "Gwen?"

She doesn't answer.

He tries her name again and again and touches her face gently, but she doesn't respond. Then he hangs his head.

"She hasn't had anything to drink," Janet says.

Dad nods.

"Is she going to be okay?" Sparky asks anxiously.

"I hope so," Dad answers, but his heart isn't in it.

It doesn't feel as chilly in the shelter as before. Maybe because of our combined body heat or maybe we're just getting used to the chill. But when Dad cranks the ventilator, Mrs. Shaw complains that it's cold.

"Who builds a bomb shelter and doesn't put warm clothes in it?" she asks in a tone Mom sometimes used when the silverware at a restaurant looked dirty.

The question looms over us in the dank, dim air. I brace myself for Dad to get angry, but he doesn't.

"I've been thinking about it, Stephanie," he replies evenly. "Maybe I never got around to putting warm clothes down here and didn't rinse the water tank or test the radio because . . . even though I built this shelter, I never wanted to believe that this could really happen."

"Then why build it in the first place?" Mr. Shaw asks.

Dad throws up his hands. "I was trying to plan for something completely illogical. Why don't you tell me, Steven. How do you apply logic to something that makes no sense?"

Mr. Shaw's forehead furrows. He looks at the floor and doesn't answer.

thirty

Mothers had breasts. When you got hurt, they would press the side of your head against their bosoms, which were sometimes soft and comforting, and sometimes rough if under their blouse they were wearing a bra, which was the thing women wore to hold their breasts in place. Boys and men didn't really have anything that needed to be held in place, except when you played Little League, you were supposed to wear a jock with a protective cup so that you didn't get whacked in the nuts by the ball.

"Watch this," Ronnie said, and crossed the street to where Paula was standing beside her bike, talking to Linda. He went behind Paula, reached for the back of her shirt, pulled something underneath, and then let go. Even across the street, you could hear the snapping sound.

Paula cried out. Her bike crashed to the sidewalk, and she ran home.

Ronnie raced back toward me. "Come on!"

I jumped up and ran after him, suspecting that he'd just done something that would get him in trouble again. At least this time, I could say I had nothing to do with it.

Old Lady Lester's backyard was a good place to hide because she stayed inside all the time. Ronnie and I sat down on the grass.

"What'd you do?" I asked.

"Snapped her bra." Ronnie grinned.

"Why?"

Ronnie stopped grinning. "That's what we're supposed to do. Girls wear bras and boys snap 'em."

"I never heard of anyone doing that before," I said.

"We didn't know any girls who wore bras before."

"My mom wears a bra."

Ronnie looked at me like I was crazy. "You can't snap your mother's bra."

"Why not?" Not that I ever would. But I mostly wanted to hear what kind of reason Ronnie would come up with.

"You just can't." He pulled up a clover and started to suck on it. "Know how to tell how big a woman's breasts are?"

"By looking at them?"

"By how thick their bra strap is."

"Why can't you tell by looking at them?"

"Sometimes you can. Sometimes you can't. It depends on what they're wearing. But you can always tell by the strap. You see a strap like this"—Ronnie spread his thumb and index finger until there was about three inches between them—"and those are really big breasts."

He paused and studied me. I stared down at the grass.

"Ever seen a breast?" he asked. "I mean, for real?"

I felt my face get hot and tugged at some hairs behind my right ear.

He gave me an astonished look. "What about your mom's?"

"She keeps them hidden."

"What about by accident? Like walking into her bedroom when she's getting dressed?"

"We're supposed to knock."

"Haven't you ever forgotten?"

"No."

Ronnie smirked. "You're allowed to forget once in a while."

"You mean . . . on purpose?" I asked, astonished.

He nodded enthusiastically. It was a shocking suggestion. Sneak into your own mother's bedroom to look at her breasts? Only someone as sick as Ronnie would think of something like that.

"You've . . . done that?" I asked.

"Of course. Every kid has."

"I've never heard of anyone doing it."

Ronnie harrumphed. "Just like you've never heard of snapping bras. Come on, you think Freak O' Nature or Johnny is going to tell the whole world he snuck into his mom's bedroom so he could look at her breasts?"

"Then how do you know?" I asked.

"I told you. Every kid does it. The best time is in the morning when she's getting dressed. Or on Saturday nights before she goes out. Moms always take baths and then try on lots of different clothes before they go out, so your chances are pretty good then."

I didn't know what to say. Sneaking looks at your mother's breasts had to be wrong.

"Scott, we could all be dead tomorrow," Ronnie said solemnly. "You want to die without ever seeing a breast?"

31

Mom can sit up if someone helps her. She'll drink and eat if you put water or food to her lips. Janet helps Dad take care of her. Sometimes Dad kneels in front of Mom and talks, but she just sits and stares blankly.

"Would you try?" Dad asks me.

I don't answer because I'm afraid. I'm not even sure what I'm afraid of.

"Come on, Scott," Dad says. "And you, too, Edward."

Sparky bites his lip and shakes his head. He's also scared.

"It's important," Dad says. "Maybe she'll recognize you."

Sparky takes my hand. He's never done that before. We face Mom.

"Say something," Dad says.

"Hi, Mom," Sparky says.

She doesn't react.

"Mom?" I say.

No response.

Sparky starts to sniff, and Dad puts his arms around him. I feel like crying, too. Now I know what I was afraid of — that she wouldn't know us, either.

Ronnie and I sit together on the bunk. Our fight is still on my mind, but most of my anger has passed. He's my best friend. Right now, he's my only friend. Maybe the only friend I'll have for the rest of my life. Before the fight, we'd never hit each other, but we'd disagreed and gotten mad plenty of times. Isn't a fistfight just more of the same?

He presses his fingertips together under his nose like a squirrel eating a nut and sniffs. Then he leans close and whispers in my ear, "Feels like jail."

He's right, with all of us crammed into this tiny room with bare gray concrete walls. I whisper back, "But *they* get more to eat."

Ronnie chuckles. The others frown when they see us whispering. Up till now, everyone's said what they're thinking out loud. And even though Ronnie and I are just talking kid stuff, I have a feeling we shouldn't look like we're sharing secrets.

I hate being hungry. I hate what's happened to my mother. I hate being down here in this smelly, chilly, damp, windowless room, with nothing to do. I hate that everyone has to go to the bathroom in front of everyone else and nobody has any privacy. I hate feeling sad about my friends and everyone else who was up there. I hate that this happened, and I hate whoever made it happen.

Dad says we should exercise. "We need to keep our strength up for what comes next."

"And just what do you think comes next?" asks Mrs. Shaw.

"Rebuilding."

Ronnie's mother rolls her eyes. "You really think life's going back to the way it used to be?"

"There won't be that much destruction outside the blast zone," Dad replies. "I think you'll be surprised."

Mrs. Shaw slowly shakes her head. "What are you going to do for food, Richard? Go to the store? There isn't going to be any food. The animals are dead. The farmers who raised them are dead. There'll be no electricity, no gasoline. If we don't starve, we'll freeze to death. Don't you understand? The world . . . has been destroyed."

"Steph, the kids," Mr. Shaw cautions.

"What difference does it make? They're going to find out soon enough," Mrs. Shaw says scornfully.

Maybe we're supposed to understand that the grown-ups are on edge, but it's still upsetting when they argue. What's even more upsetting is suspecting that Ronnie's mom is right. I tug behind my ear and glance at Sparky, who watches and listens.

"Let me tell you how you're going to spend the rest of your life, Richard," Mrs. Shaw goes on. "You'll be searching for whatever food hasn't been contaminated or gone bad. You'll be looking for clean water. You'll probably wind up migrating south, because without heat, the winters up here won't be survivable. And you want to know what's going to happen when you head south? You're going to run into all the other survivors who've had the same idea. Only then there'll be even less food and water to go around, and—"

"Dad!" Sparky cries out, and runs into his arms. "Is that true?"

"Things will be different from before," Dad says, hugging him and glaring hard at Mrs. Shaw. "But right now we don't know how."

Playing Parcheesi gets boring, so we go back to checkers. Then that gets boring, and we try Go Fish. But eventually we get to the point where we don't want to play any games at all. The boredom is bad because there's nothing to do except wonder and worry about what's going to happen next. The hunger pangs are worse, but sometimes they take my mind off the future. The bare patch behind my ear must be the size of a tennis ball, but I can't stop tugging.

Mom just sits with that blank look like a marionette with the strings cut. Sometimes I wonder if she can think but can't move her arms and legs. But she can move her eyes. Only she hardly ever does.

"I can't stand it," Mr. McGovern says. "I need to eat something."

"We'll never make it if we don't ration," Dad says.

"Then maybe we shouldn't be feeding all these mouths," says Mr. McGovern.

The words hang in the clammy air.

"What do you mean?" Dad asks.

"I think you know."

Again there's silence, as if something serious has happened. Mrs. Shaw's eyes dart from Dad to Mr. McGovern, and it feels like it does in school when a kid does something really bad. Finally, Dad says, "I think you better watch yourself, Herb."

But Mr. McGovern isn't finished. "You didn't come this far just to fail now, did you, Richard? If hunger forces us out of here too soon, it'll all be for naught."

My heart begins to thump. It sounds like Mr. McGovern is suggesting that some people leave. But who?

"We could take a simple vote," he continues. "The majority rules."

"Over my dead body," Dad says.

"You were more than willing to let people die so that you and your family could live. You'll still have your boys."

He's talking about Mom!

Dad is shaking his head in disbelief. "You can't be serious, Herb."

"I can't?" Mr. McGovern laughs bitterly. "I'm talking about survival, Richard. Isn't that what this is all about? Isn't that why you built this shelter? And in this situation, you might as well add 'of the fittest,' because like Stephanie said, that's what it's going to be once we get out of here."

"That's enough!" Dad yells, and starts pacing like a tiger in a cage. My heart beats faster, and my forehead grows hot. Are they going to fight?

Mr. McGovern turns to the Shaws. "Do *you* think it's enough? It's not as if we're guests here anymore. We're all in this together, and we all have an equal say. I think Richard's right about the food. We probably don't have enough to make it until the radiation gets down to a safe level. But with two less mouths to feed, maybe we could."

Two less mouths? Who else is he talking about? He said Dad would still have Sparky and me, and he sure

wouldn't be talking about his daughter or the Shaws. . . .
That leaves Janet.

Just a few months ago, the worst, most scary thing in life was when Dad got angry and came after me with the paddle. After that, the scariest thing was the Russians attacking. Now it's being in this bomb shelter with grown-ups arguing about who should live and die. Forget what Mrs. Shaw said about how hard life will be when we get out of here. What will happen if Mr. McGovern and the Shaws gang up on Dad? They could force Mom and Janet out, and then what would stop them from forcing Dad and Sparky and me out as well? I know Dad's stronger than either Mr. Shaw or Mr. McGovern, and I know what's in the green box on the shelf, but what if they wait until he's asleep? And they could probably make Ronnie fight me, and I'd be sure to lose.

Dad stops his tiger prowl beside Mom's bunk. "I won't hear another word of this. I said over my dead body, and I meant it." He faces Mr. McGovern. "Have you lost your mind, talking like this in front of these children? In front of this woman?" He gestures to Janet. "In front of your own daughter?" He gestures to Paula.

"To quote Charles Darwin, 'It is not the strongest of the species that survives, nor the most intelligent. It's the one that is the most adaptable to change,'" Mr. McGovern shoots back. "It looks to me like we can either adapt to the reality of this situation or starve to death."

"We're not going to die," Dad counters. "As long as we have water, we should be able to survive until the radiation levels go down."

"You hope," Mr. McGovern grouses.

Dad gives him a stern look. "Yes, Herb, I do."

thirty-two

Early each morning, the newspaper boy tossed the paper onto our driveway. Normally Dad would pick it up and read it on the train to the city, where he worked for an insurance company. But lately he went out before breakfast and brought it inside to read with Mom. Sparky and I would come into the kitchen, and they'd be sitting at the table with the paper open, coffee cups in their hands, and serious expressions on their faces.

When I asked what was going on, they either said "nothing" or gave some vague answer about the Russians and Cuba. And Mom would almost always add, "It's nothing you should worry about."

One night when Dad came in to kiss me good night, I asked, "What if the Russians attack when you're not home?"

"You'll have to go into the shelter without me."

"But what'll happen to you?"

"There are lots of shelters in the city. In the basements of buildings and the subway."

"So we could all meet again after the war?"

Dad nodded. "That's the plan."

That was good news because it meant the only times Dad might have a problem was when he was on the train going to and from work. "So if they drop the bomb and you're at work, after the war should we come to the city, or will you come back here?"

Dad ran his tongue over his front teeth and thought. "Things in New York could be pretty chaotic. You should stay out here." He got quiet for a moment. "You and Edward riding your bikes to school every day?"

I looked down at the bedcovers. A few weeks before, Dad had made us promise we would.

"I thought we agreed," he said.

"Sparky quit after the third day, and I don't like riding all the way there alone."

Dad looked off. "Well, I guess I can understand that."

"So what do we do if there's a war and we're at school?"

"Try to get home as fast as you can."

- - - - - - - -

The next day after school, I laid a wooden yardstick end over end, marking yards in chalk on the sidewalk in front of our house. When I thought I had enough, I went back and started counting them. "One, two, three."

"Seven, six, eight, twelve," Sparky began spitting out numbers until I forgot where I was. I shook my fist at him. "You want to get hurt?" He backed away and I started over, numbering each yard with chalk. I'd just finished marking off fifty yards when Ronnie and Why Can't You Be Like Johnny? came by.

Ronnie looked at the yardstick and the chalk numbers going up to fifty. Then he saw my stopwatch lying on the grass. He turned to my brother. "What's he up to?"

Sparky shook his head like he wasn't allowed to say, which was what I told him if anyone asked.

Ronnie popped a few Sugar Babies in his mouth and smacked his lips. "Man, these are good." He held the bag out to Sparky. "Want some?"

Five seconds later, Ronnie knew exactly what I was up to: trying to see how long it would take if I had to run all the way home from school.

"Scott, anyone ever tell you you're crazy?" he asked.

"Yeah. You, about a thousand times."

"Make it a thousand and one," Ronnie said. "You're crazy."

"Thanks."

"What's the point?" he asked. "Didn't you see those

pictures of Hiroshima? All those burned-up and deformed people. Why would you want to be around for that?"

"It's better than dying," I said, not because I was really sure that it was, but because it was the only answer I could think of.

"You know about radiation poisoning?" asked Why Can't You Be Like Johnny? He was in the smart class at school and never got into trouble. And he was nice. Not brownnose-teacher's-pet-nice like Paula, but nice and polite in a sincere way that made everybody like him. And if that wasn't bad enough, he was a good athlete who could throw and catch and run really fast. The only thing wrong with Why Can't You Be Like Johnny? was that there was nothing wrong with him.

"A little," I answered.

"What is it?" asked Sparky.

"It's from the radioactive fallout," Why Can't You Be Like Johnny? explained. "After the mushroom cloud, dust and ash float down out of the sky, and it's full of radiation, and when you touch it or breathe it into your lungs, it makes you sick. Your hair falls out and you throw up and—"

"Ahhhhh!" Sparky let out a cry and ran toward the house with his hands over his ears.

"Did I scare him?" asked Why Can't You Be Like Johnny?

"He has this thing about throwing up," I explained. "Even if you just mention it, he starts to cry."

"Sorry, I didn't know," Why Can't You Be Like Johnny? said. And the thing was, he wasn't just saying it. He really was sorry.

Ronnie pointed at the fifty yards I'd marked off. "You gonna try it?"

I gave him the stopwatch, then crouched down like a sprinter, pressing my hands against the rough concrete. "Anytime."

"Ready . . . set . . . go!" Ronnie yelled.

I took off as fast as I could. When I'd passed the fifty-yard line, I stopped and bent over with my hands on my thighs. "How'd I do?" I panted.

Back at the start line, Ronnie shrugged. "How would I know?"

"Didn't you time me?"

Ronnie looked down at the stopwatch. "Is *that* what this is for?"

"Very funny." I walked back to the start line, took the stopwatch, and gave it to Why Can't You Be Like Johnny? "No tricks, okay?"

Why Can't You Be Like Johnny? never played tricks on people. Once again, I crouched down. "Anytime."

"On your mark, get set, go!"

I went.

"Seven point four seconds," Johnny called out after I'd passed the finish line.

Still breathing hard, I took out a piece of paper on which I'd prepared some calculations. There were 2,640 yards in a mile and a half, and divided by 50, it was 52.8. If you multiplied 52.8 by 7.4 seconds, you got 390.72 seconds. "I can make it home in about six and a half minutes," I said.

This was good because there might be things I'd need to do before I went down into the bomb shelter. Like go into my room and get the latest *MAD* magazine if I hadn't finished reading it. And get the Halloween candy if Mom had already bought some. After all, Halloween was less than two weeks away and it would be a shame to see all that candy wasted.

"What about Sparky?" asked Ronnie.

I hadn't thought of that. Sparky was slower than me, but not that much slower. "I think he'll make it in time."

"Can I see that?" Why Can't You Be Like Johnny? gestured for the pencil and paper. I gave it to him and lay back on the grass and looked at the clouds. Today they were thin and wispy, but I was thinking about a mushroom cloud. The only picture I'd ever seen of one had looked dark gray and ominous and was no doubt filled with radioactive fallout.

"You do what we talked about?" Ronnie asked while

Why Can't You Be Like Johnny? was busy scribbling on the paper.

"Huh?"

"What we talked about after I pulled the thing that snapped? And then we ran behind Old Lady Lester's house?"

I shook my head.

Why Can't You Be Like Johnny? looked up from his calculations. "What are you talking about?"

"Nothing," I said.

"You could always look at your father's *Playboys*," Ronnie said.

"I don't think my father has any," I said.

"All fathers have *Playboys*," Ronnie insisted. "Look in his closet. If they're not there, look in his dresser drawer under his shirts."

"Does your father have *Playboys*?" I asked Why Can't You Be Like Johnny?

He shook his head and circled a number on the paper. "I hate to say this, Scott, but it's going to take you a lot longer to run home from school."

"Why?" I asked, unsettled by how he'd stressed *a lot.*

"The fastest man alive can run a mile in about four minutes. Even if he could continue at that same pace for *another* half mile, which is doubtful, it would take *him* six minutes."

"Uh-oh." Ronnie grinned. "You're probably about a

thousand times slower than the fastest man alive. If they drop the bomb while we're at school, you'll never make it home in time."

This was really bad news.

"I'd look for those *Playboys* if I were you," Ronnie said.

33

The talk of making people leave the shelter has stopped, but it doesn't feel like it's over. A little while ago, after they fed Mom, Dad put his hand on Janet's shoulder as if to reassure her that nothing bad would happen. I guess as long as we're hungry, what Mr. McGovern said will probably be in the backs of everyone's minds.

In the meantime, we have to adapt to less and less privacy. When someone has to go potty, two people hold up a sheet. It's not just for the person who's going, but for the rest of us, so we don't have to watch.

When Sparky and I go, Dad reminds us to use as little toilet paper as possible. The way he says it makes me think he's trying to remind the others as well, because he can't really tell Paula or Ronnie or the other grown-ups what to do. But with ten people, the toilet paper seems to go fast no matter how careful we are.

We quickly get used to the potty noises that made us giggle up there. If a kid in class farted, everyone would laugh and titter. But down here no one cares anymore.

Dad and Janet take Mom to the toilet bucket often in case she has to go. They turn her on her bunk so she doesn't get bedsores. Now and then Dad crouches in front of her and speaks, but he gets no reaction.

Sometimes Sparky sits next to Mom and holds her limp hand. And once in a while, he'll reach for Janet's hand. When he does that, you might catch a frown on Mr. McGovern's face. Ronnie keeps pressing his fingertips under his nose and sniffing. Paula picks her nose but tries to hide it. Mr. Shaw sticks his finger in his ear and rotates it, digging out wax. Maybe they've always done these things in public and I just never noticed, but now there's nothing else to notice. There's no outside, no windows, no TV screens. Nothing to look at but each other. There are a few books and magazines, but if someone uses the flashlight to read them, there's no light for anyone else. We take turns resting on the bunks and sitting on the floor and at the table. We've played about a million games of checkers and Parcheesi and Sorry! and Go Fish. When no one talks, we listen to the groans and cries of empty stomachs.

And I can't help wondering if we've even been down here for three days yet.

thirty-four

Once a week, Janet came to clean our house and babysit Sparky and me so that our parents could go out. She'd sleep on a cot in the laundry room and go home in the morning with a Negro man who drove a dented green car with a cracked windshield. Sometimes when Sparky and I left for school in the morning, the car would be parked in front of our house and the man would be inside it, waiting.

One afternoon back in September, I was playing with my plastic army men on the white shag carpet when Mom called, "Get in the car, kids. We're driving Janet home."

"She's not staying over?" Sparky asked.

"No, your father and I aren't going out tonight."

Mom and Janet got in the front, and Sparky and I sat in the back.

"You'll have to tell me how to get there," Mom said as we backed out of the driveway.

"I'm not exactly sure, Mrs. Porter. Elmore does the driving."

"Oh, I know," Mom said. "I'm that way when Richard drives."

It sounded strange when Mom referred to Dad by his first name. She seemed to know where to go for a while, but then we got to a corner and she stopped and glanced at Janet.

"I think it's a right turn, Mrs. Porter."

It was starting to feel like an adventure. At the next light, Mom asked, "Does this look familiar?"

Janet looked out the window and pulled her lips in. "'Fraid not, Mrs. Porter."

"I wonder if we missed a turn," Mom said. The light changed, and we had to start going again. At an Esso gas station at the next corner, Mom pulled in. "I'll be right back."

While she was in the office, a man in dark-green coveralls strolled past our car. His hands were almost black with grime and grease. When he stopped and squinted at us, Janet looked down. The man took a dirty rag out of his back pocket and wiped his hands. "Everything okay?" he asked me.

I nodded. The man glanced at Janet again and then walked toward a car waiting for gas.

Mom came out of the office and got into the car. "It's a little farther." She started to drive.

"A man asked if everything was okay," Sparky said from the back.

"Why?"

"I think because of Janet."

Janet stared down at her lap again.

"I'm sorry," Mom said.

"It's not your fault, Mrs. Porter."

I wasn't sure if Mom was sorry that Sparky had said it or sorry that the man had asked in the first place.

"Oh, there! There!" Janet suddenly got excited and pointed. "That's the street!"

Mom turned so quickly that the tires screeched, and we all slid to the right. "Aha!" She let out a gasping laugh that sounded like half relief and half surprise that the car didn't wind up on the sidewalk. Lining the street were small brick houses with white shutters. The houses were so close together that there was barely room for a driveway between them. The small yards had low metal fences and gates. In our neighborhood one lawn blended into the next, and no one had a fence. Some Negro boys around my age were playing baseball in the street, and inside a gated yard, some girls were playing teatime with dolls around a small table. The boys eyed us warily as we passed. When my friends and I played on the street, we rarely looked to see who was in the cars that went by.

"There." Janet pointed to the right. "The one with the sunflowers."

Mom pulled to the curb. Parked in the driveway was the dented green car with the cracked windshield. The hood was raised, and tools were scattered on the ground. Tall yellow sunflowers lined the yard. A tricycle lay on the grass.

Janet gathered her things. "Thank you so much for driving me home, Mrs. Porter."

"It was no bother, Janet." Mom looked at the flowers. "How pretty."

"Thank you, Mrs. Porter," Janet said as she got out. "Elmore loves to roast the seeds, but he better pick them quick before the birds get 'em."

The kids in the street were still watching us. It was hard to imagine how they could play when the balls must have constantly rolled under the parked cars that lined the curb.

Then I noticed that two small faces had come to a window in Janet's house. It felt like *High Noon* when the bad men rode into town and everyone peeked from behind curtains.

Mom started back the way we came. When we passed

the Esso station, the man in the dark green coveralls was pumping gas.

"Why did he ask if everything was okay?" Sparky said.

I expected Mom to say she didn't know, but instead she said, "That's just the way some people are, Edward."

"They don't like Negroes sitting in the same car as white people?" I asked.

Mom nodded.

"I thought that was only in the South," I said.

"I think there's a little bit of it everywhere."

35

Dad tries the radio again: nothing.

"Could it mean the Russians won?" Ronnie asks.

"Nobody won," mutters Mr. Shaw. "We destroyed them, and they destroyed us."

"Maybe not," Dad says. "Maybe Kennedy ordered our side not to retaliate."

"What are you talking about?" asks Mr. McGovern.

"There's no sense in destroying everything," says Dad.

Paula's father laughs contemptuously. "Ridiculous. He'd never let the Russians win."

"How do you know?"

"It's obvious you're no student of history, Richard." Mr. McGovern sounds like he thinks he's so smart and

Dad's so dumb. Now I know where Paula gets it. "Great men think of their place in history. They think about what they'll be remembered for. You really believe Kennedy would risk being remembered as the leader of the free world who refused to fight back? As the coward who allowed the Communists to take over? You actually think the president is hiding in a bunker somewhere waiting to surrender?"

I hate the way Mr. McGovern talks to Dad, but what I hate almost as much is how what he says sounds right. When Dad doesn't reply, I wonder if he also thinks Mr. McGovern is right.

"If the Russians did win, would we be their prisoners?" Ronnie asks.

Mr. McGovern snorts. "Just what they need. More mouths to feed. I suppose they'd need men and women for work camps, but they're no strangers to atrocities. Anyone who's familiar with their actions during the war would know that."

Sparky tugs at Dad. "What's he mean?"

"Nothing." Dad shushes him.

"Far from it," says Mr. McGovern.

Dad gets to his feet and steps toward Mr. McGovern, who is sitting with Paula. You can feel everyone grow tense. "That's it, Herb," Dad growls. "If you know what's good for you."

But Mr. McGovern doesn't look afraid. Maybe because

he knows Dad would never do anything in front of Paula and us. I almost wish he would, though.

When Janet isn't helping Mom, she sits alone and hugs her knees, staring at a spot on the floor. She hasn't been mean or done anything bad to anyone. It must be awful for her, knowing Mr. McGovern doesn't want her here.

I go sit next to her. Pulling the blanket around his skinny bare shoulders, Sparky sits on her other side and takes her hand. She sniffs and quietly starts to cry.

Sometimes Mom bought bread at the bakery, and it would still be warm on the inside. Sparky and I would spread butter and jelly on it and eat slice after slice. Sometimes she made a pizza, and we would help her press the dough out flat on the pan and cover it with tomato sauce. Sparky loved the chocolate pudding she made, but he hated the thick, gummy layer on top and would give it to me because I liked to eat it with Cool Whip. Or she'd make chocolate-chip cookies and let us eat the batter, which was always better than the cookies themselves. And at breakfast sometimes she would let us pour heavy cream over our Rice Krispies, then Sparky and I would dump sugar all over it, and it was like eating candy.

All I think about is food. I would eat anything anyone gave me right now. Even spinach.

thirty-six

In school, Dickie Keller said that in some parts of Russia they practiced cannibalism. When I got home, Mom was sitting at the kitchen table smoking a cigarette and reading an article in a magazine about decorating bomb shelters. Sparky was in the den watching TV. Recently, she'd started letting him watch all the TV he wanted. And she said I could go to Ronnie's house, even though I hadn't finished my homework.

On the floor in his room, Ronnie and I played game after game of Nok-Hockey with small wooden hockey sticks and a flat wooden puck the size of a fifty-cent piece. Ronnie won most of the time. After a while the door opened, and Mrs. Shaw came in. Her hair was all poofed up, and she had black stuff around her eyes and bright-red lips like Brigitte Bardot. "Phew!" She pinched her nose and fanned her face. "Somebody better start using deodorant."

When Ronnie lifted his arm to sniff, I saw a dark sweat stain. I felt under my arm. It was as dry as the desert.

"Scotty, your mom called," Mrs. Shaw said. "It's time for dinner."

"He can't go," Ronnie said. "We're in the middle of a huge series. If he goes now, it'll ruin everything."

That was a lie. We weren't playing a series. Ronnie just didn't want me to leave.

"I'll call her back," Mrs. Shaw said. "Maybe you can stay."

"Thanks, Mrs. Shaw."

She left, and Ronnie gave me a knowing smile. "Another game?"

While we played, I wondered how Ronnie had gotten so good at lying. When I told a lie, I really had to work at it. First I had to stop myself from telling the truth. Then I had to think of the lie I wanted to tell. Then I had to think about whether it was believable or not. Then I had to consider what would happen if I got caught. And only after all that would I dare tell it. But Ronnie was a natural. It was almost like he thought of the lie before he thought of the truth. And they were perfect lies, too. Completely believable if you didn't already know.

We were in the middle of the next game when Mrs. Shaw came in again. "Your mom says you can stay for dinner. Fried chicken, okay?"

"Great, thanks."

We must have lost track of time because the next thing I knew, the door opened, and there was Mr. Shaw in a business suit. He took a deep sniff and wrinkled his tanned forehead.

"I believe a shower will be de rigueur before you're permitted to attend tonight's soirée, my son," he said.

Sometimes Ronnie's dad had a strange way of talking, as if even he knew the words sounded funny when he said them. Like it was some kind of inside joke. Now he turned to me. "So, Scott, how about an aperitif while Sport attends to the nether regions?"

I followed him into the den, wondering what half those words meant. Everything in the Shaws' house was new and modern. Instead of white-washed wooden walls, theirs were dark and shiny. Instead of couches made of Naugahyde, which was a kind of plastic imitation leather that stuck to your skin on hot days, theirs were soft and black and made of real leather. In the den, Mr. Shaw opened a cabinet filled with shelves of glimmering glasses. "What'll it be?" he asked himself, and sorted through some bottles. "Ah! Dubonnet!" He took a bottle by the neck. "Hey, Sweet Bumps!" he called cheerfully toward the kitchen. "Wet your whistle?"

"Is the pope Catholic?" Mrs. Shaw called back.

It was like speaking a foreign language using words I knew. I heard the clink of ice in glasses and the splash of liquid. "Be right back," Mr. Shaw said, and left.

A magazine lay open on the black leather ottoman that went with Mr. Shaw's easy chair. With a jolt I realized that it had to be a *Playboy,* because there was a photo of a naked woman. How could it be just lying there, out in the open, in the middle of the Shaws' den?

The magazine was turned away, so the woman was upside down. I wanted to go over and look at her right-side up, but I was afraid that Mr. Shaw would come back and catch me.

Ronnie's dad returned and gave me a glass with ice and some deep red liquid in it. "Cheers."

We clinked glasses, and I took a sip. It tasted cold and sweet and strange. A little piece of lemon rind made it tangy. Mr. Shaw settled into his chair and propped the *Playboy* open on his lap. The cover showed the upper half of a naked woman wearing a tie, her arms crossed over her breasts. "How's that bomb shelter, Scott?"

"Dad says I'm not supposed to talk about it."

Mr. Shaw nodded. "Your parents let you drink wine?"

"No, sir."

Mr. Shaw turned a page in the magazine like it was the most natural thing in the world to give your son's friend wine and look at pictures of naked women while you chatted. "In France, children are offered wine at dinner. By the time they're teenagers, it's a natural part of life. You don't have kids going out on Friday night and getting smashed the way they do here. A much more mature and reasonable approach, don't you think?"

I took another sip and nodded.

"French women go topless at the beach," Mr. Shaw continued. "They're so much more relaxed about the human body. I mean, if a man can go around without a shirt, why can't a woman?"

I didn't know how to answer. Women going around without shirts on? Kids drinking wine? You'd think French people were the strange ones, but Mr. Shaw, sitting there thumbing through his *Playboy*, was implying that we were.

"It's time this country got past its Puritan roots," Ronnie's dad said. "This isn't the sixteen hundreds anymore; we've put men in space and broken the sound barrier. We transmit television wirelessly into people's homes and have X-rays that see through their bodies. But socially and sexually we're still back in the Stone Age."

I was tempted to tell him he was wrong because I'd seen a drawing of a caveman carrying a big club and dragging a woman around by her hair, and nobody did that anymore. By then I'd finished my drink and felt fuzzy and warm, and wished I could be alone in the den and look at the pictures in *Playboy*. Then Ronnie came in with wet hair and wearing shorts and a different shirt and said dinner was ready.

Mrs. Shaw's fried chicken came in a tinfoil tray with whipped potatoes and carrots and peas. The chicken was a little soggy, and the carrots and peas were watery, but I didn't care. They let me feed little bits of chicken to Leader, and almost everything Mr. Shaw said sounded funny and made me giggle. Later I went home, got into my pajamas, brushed my teeth, and went to bed. If Mom or Dad came in to kiss me good night, I didn't hear them.

37

We've run out of toilet paper, mostly because the women use it even when they pee. And we all pee a lot because water is the only thing we have to relieve the gnawing ache of hunger between our tiny meals.

When the air starts to feel stale and even after a deep breath you feel like you need more, it's time to use the ventilator. Dad heaves himself up and starts to crank, but after a few moments, he stops to catch his breath.

He starts again, then stops.

"What's wrong?" I ask.

"Just tired," he answers. "It's hard to keep your strength up."

"Which is *exactly* why we should eat more," Mr. McGovern says.

"Which is why it would be helpful if you took a turn," Dad counters, gesturing at the crank handle.

Mr. McGovern shakes his head. "No, thanks. I'm saving my energy."

That scares me. Is he saving energy so he can take over and kick Mom and Janet out? And then Dad, Sparky, and me after them? Mrs. Shaw gives her husband a nudge, and he reluctantly gets up. But like Dad, after a few cranks, he seems to grow tired. "Ronnie," he says.

Ronnie helps his dad crank. Together they manage to go long enough to fill the shelter with fresh air. But I feel bad. How come Dad didn't ask me to help him?

"We're like animals in a cage," Mrs. Shaw mutters. "I can't stand it."

"If you think we're like animals *now*," says Mr. McGovern, "just wait."

Mrs. Shaw pushes herself to her feet. "I have to wash. I want some water."

"It's for drinking," Dad says.

"I have to wash!" Mrs. Shaw yells. Everyone starts and stiffens. "I can't bear it," she goes on. "I feel like I'm in a dog kennel covered with filth. I'd rather die."

I glance at Mr. Shaw, expecting him to say, "Don't say that," but he just gazes at the water tank.

Mrs. Shaw's balled hands rest on her hips. "Well, Richard?"

Dad pours water into a bowl and hands her a bar of Ivory Snow. Mrs. Shaw stands over the drain in the middle of the floor and takes off her robe and nightgown.

"Don't look," Dad says. But it's impossible not to. Ronnie's mother is naked. She tears some fabric from the bottom of her robe, then dips it in the bowl of water at her feet and starts to scrub her face, neck, arms, breasts, stomach, and legs. Water and lather drip down her body, and she moans with relief as she wipes off the suds, her damp skin glistening in the dim light. Nobody says a word. Of all the eyes watching her, Ronnie's are the widest, and it makes me wonder if he ever did sneak in on her like he said he did.

By the time she finishes, she's shivering, her pale skin rubbed pink and covered with goose bumps. She considers the filmy nightgown, then tosses it aside and pulls on what's left of her robe. "I can't begin to tell you how good that felt," she says. "I feel almost human again. Anyone else want to try?"

I'm not surprised when Sparky jumps up. Shedding his blanket, he rubs the soapy rag over his front and lets Janet do his back. Like a dog being scratched, he closes his eyes as she scrubs and rinses him off, before scampering back to the blanket and huddling beside me, teeth chattering.

After that, one by one the rest of us wash. I used to hate being told to bathe; now, even with cold water, it feels like the best thing in the world.

Finally Dad and Janet lead Mom to the toilet bucket, where she seems to know what to do. Janet whispers something in Dad's ear, and he turns to us. "Don't watch."

This time I don't. Water splashes on the floor. When Janet washes her, Mom lets out a little moan like Mrs. Shaw made.

Maybe she'll be okay after all.

thirty-eight

We were playing fungo in the street in front of Ronnie's house when Puddin' Belly hit a pop-up. In right field (Ronnie's front yard), Freak O' Nature raised his mitt and backed up to catch it. Then he stopped. The ball bounced six feet to his right, but Freak O' Nature was still staring at the sky. Way, way up, three tiny silver jets were streaking across the blue, leaving white contrails. They were so high, we couldn't even hear them. I'd never seen planes that high in the sky before.

"Air force jets," said Why Can't You Be Like Johnny?

"How do you know?" asked Ronnie.

"Commercial flights don't fly that high or close together."

"Think it's war?" Freak O' Nature asked nervously.

"Wouldn't there be sirens?" I asked.

Everyone listened; there were no sirens.

"Should we get in your bomb shelter just in case?" Ronnie said.

Why Can't You Be Like Johnny? turned to Freak O' Nature. "Try your radio."

We listened. Stations were playing music or people were talking.

"Sounds pretty normal," I said.

But we kept listening, as if at any second, the sirens would start or a voice would come on the radio and tell everyone to seek shelter. Finally, Why Can't You Be Like Johnny? suggested we keep playing and check the radio again in a little while. I went back to first base (the storm drain). Johnny was playing second (chalked on the asphalt). Puddin' Belly was in left field (Old Lady Lester's front yard).

Ronnie went to home plate and was about to hit when Paula came by pushing her twin brother, Teddy, in his wheelchair. Teddy had to be strapped in and couldn't talk. His head would roll around, and he'd make strange faces and stick his fingers in his ears. Sometimes Paula would talk to him, but it was hard to tell if he understood. Sparky was afraid of Teddy, and the rest of us felt uncomfortable when he was around.

On the sidewalk, Paula locked the wheelchair's brakes

and sat down on the edge of Old Lady Lester's lawn, right in the middle of left field.

"You can't sit there!" Ronnie called from home plate.

"You don't own the sidewalk!" Paula yelled back.

"Can't you find someplace else?"

"No."

We couldn't risk hitting Teddy with the ball. Why Can't You Be Like Johnny? left second base and sat down on Ronnie's lawn, and the rest of us followed. We stared across the street at Paula and Teddy. Paula stared back.

"Want to throw rocks at her?" suggested Puddin' Belly. That was his standard solution to almost any problem.

Why Can't You Be Like Johnny? shook his head. "Just wait."

"You think if we don't play, she'll get bored and go?" asked Freak O' Nature.

"Don't bet on it," grumbled Ronnie. He and Paula had a strange relationship. They acted like they hated each other but at the same time couldn't stay away from one another.

So we looked at Paula, and she looked at us. Finally Why Can't You Be Like Johnny? went home. Then Freak O' Nature and Puddin' Belly decided to go, too. That left Ronnie and me. I didn't want to go home. Lately Mom was acting really moody, and I never knew what to expect. One minute, she'd yell at you for the littlest thing, and the next, she'd act like she didn't care what you did.

"Sneak into your mom's room yet?" Ronnie asked in a low voice.

"No."

"What about your father's *Playboy*s?"

"What do you care?"

Ronnie glanced across the street at Paula, then whispered, "Just hate to think of you dying without ever seeing—"

"I'm not gonna die, remember? I'm the one with the bomb shelter, and I'll be in there for weeks with my mom and get to see everything."

"You might not," Ronnie said. "Might be pretty dark. It's not like you'll have electricity."

Like a dog on the other end of a stick, he wouldn't let go.

"And moms don't really count because you can't do anything with them," he said. "Wouldn't you like to see some you could do something with?"

"Do what?"

"You don't know?" Ronnie asked in that tone that always made me feel like I was stupid.

"Go to hell."

"Keep it down," Ronnie mumbled, and glanced across the street again. "If you could see any pair of breasts in the whole world, whose would you want to see?"

"How would I know?"

"Paula's, right?" he whispered.

The thought had never occurred to me. Paula might have had breasts, but she was also our neighbor and the annoying teacher's pet who always raised her hand in class.

"No," I said.

"Yes, you do."

"No . . . I . . . don't."

Ronnie studied me. "You a homo?"

"A what?"

"A homo. A queer."

"No."

"Sure you are. Any guy who doesn't care about breasts has to be queer."

"No, you don't," I said. "What do breasts have to do with it?"

Across the street, Paula got up and started to push Teddy back home. Maybe she'd decided there was no point in being there if we weren't going to pay attention to her. "You don't even know what queer is," Ronnie sneered.

"Yes, I do."

"No, you don't."

"Do, too."

"Oh, yeah? Then what is it?"

"It's . . . it's you know, when you're, you know, kind of strange and different."

Ronnie's grin grew broader. "You don't know what *queer* means," he sang, like it was a line from a song.

"That's what it means," I insisted.

"No, it doesn't," Ronnie said. "It means you like other guys."

I studied him uncertainly. I liked my friends — most of the time, at least — and they were guys. What was queer about that?

Ronnie saw the confusion on my face. "Queers are guys who have sex with other guys. They're called homos because they're homosexuals."

I smiled. There was no way Ronnie was going to get away with this one. "Guys can't have sex with guys. It's not even possible, stupid."

But Ronnie smiled back. "What rock have you been hiding under?"

It didn't make sense. Men and women had body parts that fit together. Men couldn't have sex with men because they had the same body parts and therefore wouldn't fit.

"So how do they do it?" I asked.

Ronnie shook his head like he knew the answer and didn't want to tell.

"Come on, if you're so smart, let's hear it," I said.

"I would, but if your parents found out, they'd be really mad."

"I swear to God I won't tell them."

"How do I know you'll keep your promise?"

I held out my right pinkie, and Ronnie stopped smiling. A pinkie swear was the most inviolate swear there was. If you broke a pinkie swear, you were branded for life. No one would ever trust you again.

"Come on." I beckoned with my outstretched pinkie. Ronnie didn't take it.

"See?" I said. "You're such a liar."

39

"I'm hungry." Sparky crosses his arms over his stomach and bends forward like he's in agony. Even before this, he was skinny and bony, but now his ribs poke out, especially where the concave curve of his stomach begins.

"There, there." Janet puts her arm around his shoulders and tries to soothe him. He sits with her almost all the time now.

"Give him something," Mrs. Shaw says to Dad.

"What about my child?" asks Mr. McGovern.

Hunger has turned my stomach into a knot, too, and my own ribs feel tight against my skin, but I don't want to say anything that will make it worse for Dad, who goes over to the shelf. "Sardines?"

Sparky shakes his head.

"Tuna?"

"Okay."

"Why does he get to choose when the rest of us don't?" Mr. McGovern asks.

"If your child was the youngest here, I'd do the same for her," Dad answers.

"But not if she's the second or third youngest?"

"That makes no sense, Richard," Mrs. Shaw says. I hate the way she and Mr. McGovern gang up on Dad. It's still our bomb shelter and our food. Like Dad said, they could have built their own shelters.

"I'm hungry, too," says Ronnie.

"What's left?" asks Mrs. Shaw.

Mr. Shaw hardly talks anymore. Mostly he just stares at the walls and floor. It makes me uncomfortable. He seems like a different person from the one who sat in his den sipping wine and talking about topless women in France.

Dad tells us what remains on the food shelf. "Three cans of Spam, four of tuna, six of sardines, and some peanut butter and jelly."

"No bread?" asks Mrs. Shaw.

Dad shakes his head.

"We could make it last longer," Mr. McGovern says. "For someone hardheaded and logical enough to build this shelter, you've become awfully softhearted, Richard."

Dad glares at him furiously. "You're talking about my wife and this innocent woman, Herb."

"I'm talking about our lives and the lives of our children," Mr. McGovern replies forcefully. "We've already lost enough thanks to this goddamn war. The sooner we use up the food, the sooner we'll be forced to go back up there. And if we go up too soon, we run the risk of radiation sickness. Be rational about it, Richard. It's not going to get any easier once we're up there. Like Stephanie said, we'll be spending every moment trying to survive. There won't be time for anyone who needs help."

"How can you say that?" Dad asks. "I mean, think of your own son."

Mr. McGovern's face darkens. "That . . . is *exactly* why I can say it."

I feel the urge to tug. The spot behind my right ear feels as smooth and hairless as my forehead, but along the edge of the bald spot, I find some hairs to grasp. Mr. McGovern doesn't think we'll be able to take care of Mom once we get out, but why does he want Janet to leave? Because she's a Negro? If he makes her leave, what's to stop him from saying Sparky should go next? After all, he's too young and small to take care of himself.

"So?" Mr. McGovern demands.

Dad gathers himself up. "I said it before and I'll say it again. Over . . . my . . . dead . . . body."

"It won't just be *your* dead body—it will be

everyone's," Mr. McGovern counters, then turns to the Shaws. "Who gave him the right to make decisions for all of us? Because it's his bomb shelter? I'm sorry, but I don't think that matters anymore. We're all in this together now. Are you really comfortable putting your lives in *his* hands? Letting *him* decide how much we eat and drink?"

Mrs. Shaw glances at her husband, who's staring at a wall as if his thoughts are a million miles away. Then she says in a softer, more reasonable tone, "Let the children eat, Richard."

"I never said I wasn't going to," Dad replies icily. He opens a can of tuna and divides it four ways. Normally I could eat my share in one bite, but I separate it into three parts and savor each one slowly.

Sparky gets to lick the inside of the can.

When I finish my three parts, I'm still hungry.

Sometimes, when it's quiet for a long time, I think I hear whispers, as if there's someone else down here. And even though I don't believe in ghosts, I get scared. If I never imagined the whole world being destroyed, what else have I never imagined? Could there be some kind of invisible radioactive creature on the other side of the shield wall? Invisible Godzilla?

I look over at Mom, wishing she would wake up so I could tell her about Invisible Godzilla and she could tell me it's only my imagination. But she just lies there, blank-eyed, so I go over to Janet and hold her hand. If Mr. McGovern and the Shaws say she has to go, I'll say over my dead body, too.

When we run out of rags for washing and the toilet, the men tear off their pajama legs at the knees. We're slowly using up our clothing.

At times the hunger and the feeling of being cooped up in this chilly, smelly dungeon is so bad, I feel like I can't spend another minute down here. Would it be worth risking radiation poisoning to go up and see the sun for a few minutes? Could such a short time up there be *that* bad?

Dad and Mr. McGovern have an argument over how long we've been down here. Dad thinks it's only been five or six days. Mr. McGovern insists it's been eight or nine.

"This is more than a week's worth of beard," Mr. McGovern says, brushing the stubble that mats the lower half of his face. The lower half of Dad's face is similarly darkened, but Mr. Shaw's is only patchy, and I wonder if he could grow a beard even if he wanted to.

"Maybe it's time to check the radiation levels again," Mrs. Shaw says in her nice voice.

Dad starts to get to his feet, then stumbles and has to grab the bunk bed.

"Dad!" Sparky blurts with fright.

"Sorry, just got a little dizzy."

"Hunger," Mr. McGovern grumbles as if it's Dad's fault.

When Dad picks up the flashlight, Sparky whimpers. Janet presses the side of his head to her bosom and comforts him. "He'll just be gone for a moment."

At the shelf lined with supplies, Dad aims the flashlight beam at the green box as if he's thinking about what's inside. Then he takes the Family Radiation Measurement Kit and goes into the corridor on the other side of the shield wall. Once again without the flashlight, it gets darker in the shelter. Then he's back. "A hundred and sixty roentgens."

"Isn't that much better than before?" Mrs. Shaw asks hopefully.

Dad nods grimly. "It's still much too high."

There's nothing on the radio.

"I guess the good news is you're not picking up any stations in Russian," says Mr. McGovern.

"I'd almost feel better if we did," mumbles Mr. Shaw. It feels like it's the first time he's spoken in days.

Ronnie scowls at his dad. "Why?"

"At least we'd know someone was out there," Mr. Shaw replies.

Mr. McGovern, who always has to have the last word, mutters, "Better dead than red."

forty

"Take cover! We're under attack!" We were in the middle of learning ratios when Principal Sharp's voice crackled over the PA system: "Follow your teacher's instructions! Duck and cover! Duck and cover!"

Puddin' Belly Wright ran to the windows. A few weeks earlier, Principal Sharp had told each teacher to select a student to pull down the window shades so we wouldn't be blinded or burned by the nuclear flash. It sounded like an important job, but Mr. Kasman chose Puddin' Belly, who now pulled a shade so hard that the whole thing came crashing down.

"Ahh!" Paula wailed.

"Oh, for Christ's sake," Mr. Kasman sputtered.

Kids dove for the floor.

"Stop!" Mr. Kasman shouted. "It's not an attack. It's just a drill."

"But Principal Sharp said —"

"Be quiet," our teacher ordered. "Do you hear sirens?"

We listened. There were no sirens.

"Why did Principal Sharp say we were under attack?" asked Freak O' Nature.

Instead of answering, Mr. Kasman closed his eyes and squeezed the bridge of his nose with his fingertips as if he was getting a headache.

"Should we still get under our desks?" Ronnie asked.

Our teacher took his hand away from his face. "Sure, go ahead." He sounded like he didn't care.

It wasn't easy. Our new desks came with chairs that were attached. We were crawling around on the floor, trying to get under them, when the PA crackled back on. "Uh, there's been some confusion," said Principal Sharp. "We are not under attack. I repeat, we are not under attack. This is an air-raid drill. I repeat, this is only a drill. Teachers, escort your students into the hallway and await further instructions."

"You heard him," said Mr. Kasman. "Everyone out to the hall."

We wiped our dirty hands on our pants and filed out. Up and down the corridor, kids were pouring from classrooms. Some of the girls were red-eyed and teary, and some boys looked pale and shaken — as if their teachers had believed it was a real attack, too.

"Students, sit with your backs against lockers, your knees pulled up, and your faces buried in your arms," Principal Sharp announced over the loudspeaker.

"Do as he said," instructed Mr. Kasman.

"I have ordered you out into the hall because in the event of a nuclear attack, this will protect you from flying glass and flash burns," Principal Sharp continued. "You will keep your eyes shut and covered to prevent blindness from the flash. No matter where you are, do not look at the blast. Always turn your back to it and look away."

"Always," Mr. Kasman repeated.

41

The hunger pangs have gone from sharp to dull but constant. Everyone's irritable. Ronnie's winning a game of Parcheesi until Sparky rolls a six and knocks one of his pawns back to the start.

"Why'd you do that?" Ronnie asks. "You could have used that roll to get your pawn home."

"I can do that later," Sparky replies.

"Why not now?" Ronnie asks.

"If I don't send your pawn back, you'll win."

"No, I won't," Ronnie says, which is dumb because he wants to win and getting all your pieces home is how you do it.

"Sure you will," I tell him.

"Maybe not," Ronnie says. "Maybe I would have slowed down just to make it interesting."

"So Sparky did that for you," I chip in.

"It wasn't the right move."

"He can make any move he wants," I tell him.

"He would have been better off going home."

"But then you would have won."

"I quit." Ronnie flips a corner of the board, and pawns go rolling everywhere.

That ticks me off. "You're just mad because you thought you were going to win and then Sparky messed you up."

"You're stupid."

"I may be stupid, but even my little brother's smarter than you."

"Oh, yeah? Well, your dad's so dumb, he didn't put enough food or clothes in here."

Silence. Dad winces.

"Ronnie!" Mrs. Shaw snaps, which is a little surprising because she said the same thing about dad a few days ago.

"Well, it's—" Ronnie begins, but doesn't finish. Not that it matters. Everyone knows he was going to say it's true.

I wonder if Dad will get mad, but he bows his head. "He's right. I could've done better. I *should* have. I mean, what was the point of building this shelter and then leaving the job unfinished?"

That's the thing about Dad. Maybe he isn't as smart as Mr. McGovern or as suave as Mr. Shaw, but when he realizes he's wrong, he admits it. Not a lot of parents do that. Kids, either. Mrs. Shaw must feel bad about being so critical of him because now she says, "You did just fine, Richard. If it wasn't for you, none of us would be alive."

"Whoop-dee-do!" Mr. Shaw goes, like he doesn't think being alive is so great.

"Steven!" Mrs. Shaw hushes him, as if instead of being angry at Dad, she's now angry at him.

Mr. Shaw goes back into silent mode, but it's scary to see him act like he's giving up. What if he's right?

forty-two

When the leaves began to fall, Dad bought a lawn sweeper. It had four long brushes on a rotating drum followed by a leaf catcher. You pushed it across the lawn, which made the drum rotate and the brushes turn, sweeping up leaves into the catcher.

I had to sweep the whole lawn, which was hard work. But when I'd dumped a few loads at the curb and had a good-size pile, I was allowed to pour gasoline on the leaves and light them. Fires were great entertainment.

I'd just made a big pile when Freak O' Nature rode up on his bike and told me not to burn them until he came back. A little later, he returned with Ronnie and a jar filled with crickets. I got the red gasoline can from the garage and sprinkled some on the leaves.

"That's all?" Ronnie asked.

"You don't need a lot," I said. "Leaves pretty much burn by themselves."

"Put some more on," Ronnie said, so I did.

"More," he urged.

The leaves glistened and the odor of gasoline was strong in the air. I carried the can far away, then returned, pulling a pack of matches out of my pocket. Normally I'd crouch down and light a few leaves, then wait for the flames to reach the gas. But now there was gas every-where. It had even started to seep from the leaves and spread onto the street.

Freak O' Nature spun the lid off the jar and dumped the crickets onto the pile. Some started to hop away on the street. Others landed on the gasoline-soaked leaves and seemed stunned.

"Do it!" Ronnie yelled.

I stood back and tossed a lit match toward the pile, but it went out before it hit the leaves. I lit another and tossed it, but the same thing happened. Meanwhile, more crickets were getting away.

"Gimme that." Ronnie grabbed the matches and crouched close to the pile.

Whoomp!

I could have sworn that for an instant Ronnie disappeared in the eight-foot-high ball of flames. The initial burst quickly died down; the crackling leaves burning rapidly, turning bright red and then into ashes. Crickets jumped around frantically in the orange and yellow flames before being immolated. A few even managed to launch themselves, burning, to the pavement, where they kicked once or twice, then lay still, tiny carcasses and smoke.

My friends and I took in the charred devastation. The smoldering heap of gray ash, the wisps of smoke rising like ghosts. All that remained of the crickets were burned carapaces, except for a few dead ones that had managed to hop away before the fire began, only to be poisoned by the gasoline.

"Just like what could happen to us," Ronnie said.

43

When Dad turns the valves, more water gurgles into the tank. "Looks like you were right," he tells Mr. McGovern.

Paula's father nods like he knew he was right all along.

"Then no one else survived," Mr. Shaw mutters.

"Certainly very few," Mr. McGovern agrees.

"How do you know?" asks Mrs. Shaw.

Mr. McGovern explains how water towers are built to hold about a day's worth of water for the population they serve. "So, if we've been down here nine or ten days . . ."

"Or six or seven," says Dad.

"Whatever the number," Mr. McGovern says irritably, "it must mean very few people are using it."

Is it day up there? Night? What day of the week? How many more days do we need to stay down here? Sometimes if I think about it too hard, I feel queasy like after a roller-coaster ride. Mr. McGovern says without knowing day from night that we've become disoriented.

Nobody plays games anymore. It takes too much energy. We sit, or lie down, or sleep. Sometimes someone stands up because they can't sit anymore.

I think about Tootsie Rolls, Milky Ways, Frosted Flakes, Rice Krispies, Pop-Tarts, Premium Saltines, Oreos, Wise Potato Chips, Fritos, peanut butter and jelly sandwiches, milk shakes, hamburgers, Chinese food, spaghetti, pizza, sweet-and-sour meatballs . . .

My stomach churns and cries. Sometimes drinking water helps, but sometimes it doesn't. The air is always stuffy. We take turns cranking the ventilator, but no one has the strength to crank it more than three or four times. So there isn't enough food and barely enough air. But that's not the scariest part of being down here. The scariest part is the way the grown-ups act.

"Check the radiation," Mr. McGovern says. He no longer bothers to ask.

"I just checked it a few hours ago," Dad replies.

"That was yesterday, Richard."

"No, Herb, it was today."

Mr. Shaw sighs. "What does it matter?"

"Anything would be better than being down here," Mr. McGovern says.

"You can leave anytime you like," Dad snaps.

"I'm not the one who should leave." Mr. McGovern's eyes seem full of anger and hatred. Is that what he saved his energy for?

"I told you I won't have that," Dad growls.

"Who made you the commander in chief?" Mr. McGovern turns to Mrs. and Mr. Shaw. "I say we vote on reducing the number of mouths by two. This isn't arbitrary — it's a matter of survival. It's what has to be done if we're going to stay down here long enough to let the danger subside up there."

Janet's eyes go wide. As if my stomach doesn't already hurt enough, now it twists and knots even more.

Is Dad too tired to argue? When he moves close to the shelves and places his hand near the green box, I feel my heart begin to thump hard and my breaths grow short and fast. He can't be serious. This can't be happening.

But that's what they said about a war with the Russians in the first place.

Mr. McGovern finishes his speech. "All those in favor of reducing the number of mouths by two, raise your hands."

Dad rests his hand on the green box.

Mr. McGovern raises his hand and looks at the Shaws. Neither of them budges.

A scowl darkens Mr. McGovern's face. "Even though we'll die if we have to go up there too soon?"

"I told you before," says Mrs. Shaw. "I'd rather die than be responsible for someone else's death."

"Steven?" Mr. McGovern says.

Mr. Shaw slowly shakes his head. "Up there, down here. What difference does it make?"

forty-four

Despite the duck-and-cover drills and talk about a nuclear war, teachers still had to teach. In current events, Mr. Kasman reminded us that there were other things going on in the world. He wrote "James Meredith" on the board. "Does anyone know who this man is?"

No one answered.

"James Meredith recently became the first colored man ever to enroll in the University of Mississippi," our teacher said.

Paula's hand shot up. "They didn't want to let him in."

"That's right," said Mr. Kasman.

Paula grinned proudly, as if to say, *See how smart I am?* But if she was really so smart, how come she wasn't in the smart-kid class with Why Can't You Be Like Johnny?

"And can you tell us who 'they' are, Paula?" Mr. Kasman asked.

Paula stopped smiling. "Uh, some . . . white people?" she asked more than stated.

"Yes." Mr. Kasman nodded, and Paula looked relieved. But not for long. "You're white, Paula. Would you have been against James Meredith going to the University of Mississippi?"

Paula's eyes darted around nervously. "No . . . "

"Then why do you think those people in Mississippi were against him going?"

Paula didn't answer, and no hands went up. Except for school custodians and cleaning ladies, we hardly ever came into contact with Negro people. I thought about Janet and the three men who'd dug the hole in our backyard.

"Who knows what segregation is?"

Once again, Paula's hand shot up. "It's when white people and Negroes are kept separate."

"Why?" asked Mr. Kasman. It was strange the way he asked us questions instead of just telling us stuff. As if he actually wanted to know what we thought. I couldn't remember a teacher doing that before. Miss Yellnick, my fifth-grade teacher, always acted like the last thing she wanted to know was what we thought. After all, we were kids. How were we supposed to know the answers? But the funny thing was, asking us made us think, whereas half the time when teachers told us stuff, it just went in one ear and out the other.

"In some parts of the South, there are separate restaurants for whites and Negroes," said Mr. Kasman. "There are separate water fountains and bathrooms. Negroes have to ride in the back of public buses."

"Back of the bus," Freak O' Nature rumbled in a deep low voice like the Kingfish's on the TV show *Amos 'n' Andy.* Some kids giggled.

Mr. Kasman ignored him and waited. You could feel discomfort spread through the classroom. What was he waiting for?

"Okay." He seemed to make up his mind. "Here's part of your homework for tonight. I want each of you to write a page answering this question." He turned to the blackboard and wrote: "Why would someone be against letting a Negro go to an all-white university? And do you agree or disagree with that position?"

A bunch of us groaned, but then we always groaned when Mr. Kasman gave us homework.

That night I wrote:

I think people who are against letting a Negro
go to an all-white university probably think that

Negroes shouldn't go to college because they were once slaves. I think this is wrong because Negroes are not slaves anymore.

It is wrong for people to be against letting a Negro go to an all-white university because they think that Negroes shouldn't go to college because they were once slaves. I think those people should think about how they would feel if Negroes had made white people slaves instead of the other way around. I don't think white people would like it one bit if they wanted to go to an all-Negro college and weren't allowed. The golden rule says we should do unto others as they would do unto us.

In conclusion, it is wrong for white people to be against letting a Negro go to an all-white university because they think that Negroes shouldn't go to college because they were once slaves.

45

"The refuse can is almost full," Dad says.

"So, what do you suggest, Herr Kapitän?" asks Mr. McGovern, as if he's hoping maybe this could be another reason to reduce the number of mouths by two.

"Oh, am I still in charge?" Dad asks sarcastically.

"Suppose we just put the solid waste in it?" Mrs. Shaw asks.

Dad nods. "That's what I was thinking."

So now liquid waste goes directly into the drain on the floor. The men stand; the women squat. People don't always hold up the blanket for privacy anymore. It takes too much energy. The men just turn their backs and go. Janet and Mrs. Shaw hold the blanket for Paula. Dad and Janet take Mom by the arms and help her to squat. Seeing people go now, I feel the way I used to feel when one of our neighbors' dogs went. What's the big deal?

Why was it ever a big deal?

Out of the blue, Mr. Shaw says, "We're worse than animals. Animals only kill what they need for food. Humans kill for no reason."

Eyes shift as we glance at one another. No one replies.

Dad tries the radio. "There've got to be others. Sooner or later, someone has to start broadcasting."

"Powered by what?" Mr. McGovern sighs like parents do when their kids act stubbornly. "You think the power plants are still standing? And even if they are, you think the people who run them are still alive? And they're just going to go back to work? What's the point? To earn a salary? Who's going to pay them? And even if someone did, what would they do with the money? Go to a store? There's nothing to buy. No one's going back to work, Richard. No one's making anything. They're all too busy just trying to survive."

"The government made contingency plans," Dad counters. "They stored food and gasoline. The army'll get things going again."

Mr. McGovern rolls his eyes. "You've been completely brainwashed. Do you have any idea how much food and fuel it takes to keep this country running? It doesn't matter what the government has stored. Without a constant supply of new coal, oil, and natural gas, whatever they've got won't last more than a month or two. So unless the army is going to start mining and drilling, and processing and refining, and transporting, and running power plants, it can't possibly go back to the way it was."

Nobody argues. Dad has his listening-and-thinking face on.

"And I'll tell you something else," Mr. McGovern continues. "Our power plants and refineries were probably the first things the Russians bombed. Just like their power plants and oil fields were the first things we bombed. And it's not like we can rebuild whatever was damaged; anything that got a direct hit from a nuclear weapon will be radioactive for decades, if not centuries. So to have the energy we need means digging new mines and oil wells, as well as building new power plants. How long do you think *that* will take?"

Dad doesn't answer.

"How long?" asks Sparky.

"Not in our lifetimes," Mr. McGovern answers, still focusing on Dad. "Maybe now you can understand why some of us weren't in a hurry to build bomb shelters."

He makes it sound like it's going to be really awful when we go back up there. Almost like, as horrible as it is down here, we might be better off staying. Meanwhile, Dad turns to Paula's father.

"You know, Herb," he says. "In some ways, you're a very smart guy, but in other ways, you're one of the stupidest people I've ever met."

In the shadows of our dungeon, tension once again begins to spread. I've never heard a grown-up call another grown-up a name before. Certainly not to his face. And not only that, but I never thought Dad would be the one to do it.

At first, Mr. McGovern clenches his teeth. But then he seems to relax and even smiles. "All right, Richard, perhaps you'd like to tell us what makes you say that."

"You fought to get in here because when faced with death, you realized how precious life is," Dad says. "I can't imagine how horrible it must have been to leave your wife and son up there, but you made that choice. We all did, or we wouldn't be down here. None of us really knows what it's going to be like when we get back up there. In the meantime, all we've got to keep us going is hope. But you're so damn intent on proving to everyone how smart you are that you don't seem to care that you're destroying the last bit of hope the rest of us are clinging to. So from now on, keep it to yourself."

But we know who always has to have the last word. "According to Nietzsche," Paula's father replies, "'In reality, hope is the worst of all evils, because it prolongs man's torments.'"

forty-six

Dad brought home a brown-paper shopping bag with handles made from bamboo and wire.

"What is it?" Sparky asked eagerly.

"I'll show you after dinner," Dad said. That always drove Sparky and me crazy. Maybe it was supposed to teach us patience, but all it really did was make us rush through meals.

To make things worse, Mom served spinach. Except for canned asparagus, there was nothing Sparky and I hated more. But dinner couldn't end until we finished it. I put lots of butter on mine and managed to eat most of it. About halfway through the meal, Sparky got up to go to the bathroom.

He didn't come back.

After a while, Dad said, "Go see what Edward's doing."

As I went down the hall to the bathroom, I heard the toilet flush. Then it flushed again. I knocked.

"Who is it?" Sparky asked.

"Me," I said in a low voice. "What's going on?"

Sparky peeked out, then let me in and locked the door. In the toilet were a million little green pieces of spinach. "I spit it out," he whispered, "but it won't flush."

This was bad. If Mom or Dad found out that Sparky had filled his mouth with spinach and then spit it out, we might not get to see what Dad brought home. I flushed the toilet. The water swirled around and disappeared, then reappeared with most of those little green pieces of spinach still there.

Rap! Rap! The knock on the door made us both jump. "Boys?"

Sparky's eyes went wide.

"Open the door," Dad ordered.

Sparky and I shared a frightened look. As I opened the door, Sparky quickly put down the toilet top and sat. Dad scowled at us. "What's going on?"

"We were just talking," Sparky said.

"With the door locked?" Dad asked.

"It was boy stuff," I said.

Dad frowned. "Well, come on and see what I got."

As we followed Dad down the hall, Sparky rolled his eyes in relief. In the bedroom, Dad took four olive-colored masks out of the shopping bag. Each was about the size of a football with U.S. NONCOMBATANT GAS MASK stenciled in black letters on the outside. They were made of rubber with two clear plastic see-through disks. At one end was a gray canister about the size of a Campbell's soup can. At the other end were straps. Sparky put one on, instinctively knowing that the straps went around the back of his head and the clear plastic disks went where his eyes were. He looked like a green anteater with the gray can for a snout. I followed his example. Dad tightened the straps until the gas masks felt firm on our heads. The air inside quickly became warm and stale.

"What's it for?" I asked, my voice muffled by the mask.

"So you won't breathe in radioactive fallout," Dad said.

Mom came in. When she saw Sparky and me, she frowned.

"They're gas masks, Mom!" Sparky announced with muffled excitement.

Mom crossed her arms and said to Dad, "Scaring them again?"

"We're not scared," Sparky said. But then he turned to me and asked uncertainly. "Are we?"

"I'm not scared," I said, because I didn't want Dad to get into trouble.

"You better take those off," Dad said.

"And go watch TV," added Mom, in a way that indicated that Dad was in trouble anyway.

We went into the den and watched *Sky King*, but I could hear the sounds of an argument coming from Mom and Dad's bedroom. Sparky's eyes were fixed on the TV; I got up and quietly went down the hall to listen.

"The whole town's talking," Mom said. "They stare at me in the store. I can feel their eyes."

"I'm sorry," Dad said. "But I can't sit here and do nothing. Even President Kennedy said we should build a shelter. He's building one at his summer place in Hyannis Port, and we all know there's got to be an enormous shelter in Washington."

"Well, good for him. Meanwhile, Scott's pulling the hair out of his head and is so worried he threw up his dinner."

"What?"

I had to get closer to try to hear what Mom said next. Suddenly the door swung open. Dad looked startled when he saw me. "You . . . were listening?"

I bowed my head in shame.

"You threw up?"

"Ahhhh!" Halfway down the hall, Sparky let out a cry and dashed away. He must have been coming to see what we were talking about.

"I'll take care of him." Mom went past us.

In a low voice, I told Dad that I hadn't thrown up, but that Sparky had been so eager to see what was in the shopping bag that he'd filled his mouth with spinach and spit it out in the toilet. Dad sighed, then reached out and turned my head with his hand. "What's this?"

"I don't know."

"You pull out hair when you're worried?"

I nodded.

"Try not to, okay?"

47

In order to have toilet paper and washcloths, we've torn our nightclothes down to almost nothing. Paula and Janet clutch what remains of their robes tightly when they move around, but Mrs. Shaw can't be bothered and lets her shredded robe hang open, revealing the nakedness beneath. I guess she knows that we're all so hungry, weak, and miserable that no one cares.

"I can't stand it!" Mr. Shaw suddenly pushes himself up. It seems like the first time he's stood up in days, although that probably isn't true. He stumbles toward the gap in the shield wall.

"What are you doing?" Mrs. Shaw gasps.

"I'll take my chances up there."

"Dad!" Ronnie dashes after his father and wraps his arms around one of his legs.

Shock and alarm fill the shelter. For an instant, my dad looks dumbfounded. Then he hoists himself up and grabs Mr. Shaw's arm.

"Let go!" Mr. Shaw tries to yank free.

"You'll kill us all!" Dad warns.

"I can't stay in here anymore!"

"Dad, stop!" Ronnie cries as his father tries to drag him.

"You're scaring him, Steven!" Mrs. Shaw yells.

With Ronnie's arms wrapped around his thigh like a boa constrictor, Mr. Shaw tries to squirm out of Dad's grip in a strange slow-motion dance as if they don't have the strength to move faster. Dad hooks an arm around Mr. Shaw's neck, and they tumble to the shelter floor, a mass of squirming arms and legs.

"Let go!" On the floor, Mr. Shaw tries to wriggle and twist away, but Ronnie's still clamped to his leg, and Dad manages to pin his arms down. Ronnie's crying and Mrs. Shaw is yelling, "Stop it! Stop it!" Mr. Shaw twists his head back and forth and tries to kick with his free leg. "Let me go!"

But Dad has him pinned. "If you open that door now, the radioactive dust that falls in could kill us all."

Her hair a wild mess, Mrs. Shaw kneels and takes her husband's head in her hands. "Stop," she says gently but firmly. "Get ahold of yourself. I understand how you feel. I really do. But you have to think about the rest of us. Ronnie needs you. I need you."

Her words get through. Mr. Shaw goes limp. The back of his head rests on the floor, and he bursts into tears, hiccupping and snorting, his chest heaving.

I've never seen a grown man cry so publically before, and it feels strange and upsetting. Sparky's whimpering. Janet strokes his head reassuringly. Paula's eyes are wide as she clings to her father. We're all so close together; there's nowhere to hide. Ronnie lets go of his father's leg and sits on the floor, wiping his eyes, his face smudged with tears and dirt.

Mrs. Shaw helps her husband to one of the bunks and lies down with him. She kisses his face and whispers in his ear. He slides his arms around her and pulls her close. I feel bad that they can't be alone.

Dad watches Mrs. Shaw caress and soothe her husband. He turns his gaze to Janet hugging Sparky. Then he looks at Mom, lying on her bunk with that blank expression, not the slightest bit aware of what just happened.

Dad doesn't check the radio anymore. But whenever he wakes up from a nap, he goes around the shield wall and tests the radiation levels under the trapdoor.

"A hundred and twenty-seven," he reports.

It's dropped again, but is still high above the safe level. Meanwhile, we're slowly starving to death.

forty-eight

On the TV, President Kennedy wore a dark jacket, white shirt, and thin black tie. He sat at a desk with a dark curtain and an American flag behind him.

The president had a funny way of speaking that had something to do with being from an important Massachusetts family. He said that the Soviets had given false statements about their weapons. The Soviets was another name for the Russians, who were also called Commies, Ruskies, and Reds. The president said that the Soviets were putting two types of weapons on Cuba — medium-range ballistic missiles that could reach Washington and intermediate-range missiles that were capable of reaching Hudson Bay in Canada. Sparky glanced at me with a scowl. Our parents had once gone to Canada for a vacation and came back with Hudson Bay blankets, and I bet he was wondering why the Soviets would want to shoot a missile all the way up there . . . unless they had something against blankets.

The president said the missiles were weapons of mass destruction and that the Soviets were lying about why they were putting them on Cuba. He used a lot of big words, and when he said a quarantine of Cuba was going to be initiated, I wanted to ask Dad what that meant, but I knew he'd tell me to wait until the speech was over.

When the president began talking about the organ of consultation and the Rio Treaty, Sparky started playing with a Slinky. I was tempted to play with my army men, but I watched mostly to see if the president would explain what the Commies had against Hudson Bay and what a quarantine was.

Then Mom came in. I had a feeling that she'd stayed out of the den on purpose to let Dad know that she was against Sparky and me watching the speech, but now she finally gave in to curiosity. She stood with her arms crossed while President Kennedy said that many months of sacrifice and self-discipline lay ahead, and that the cost of freedom was always high and one thing we would never do is surrender. Then he said, "Thank you and good night," and the speech was over.

I looked at Dad. "When he talked about the cost of freedom, he wasn't talking about money, was he?"

Dad sighed and shook his head.

"Maybe we shouldn't go to school tomorrow," I whispered to Dad at bedtime that night. Sparky was already asleep in the other bed.

Dad's forehead wrinkled. "Why?"

"If the Russians attack, we may not have time to get home."

Dad leaned forward and kissed me on the forehead. "Go to school and don't worry so much."

But it was impossible not to.

49

Everyone's sick. The air smells tart and pungent, and there's hardly a moment when someone isn't sitting on the toilet bucket. I feel dizzy and hot with a cramped stomach that's different from the cramps that come from hunger. For the first time in days, I don't think about food or even getting out of the shelter. I just want to stop feeling sick.

By now, the men have torn their pajama tops into rags, but there's still not enough. Dad is the first one to take off his pajama bottoms. Only there isn't any material around for Janet to make him a loincloth the way she did for Sparky.

We nap, wake, sit on the toilet bucket, and lie around feeling too ill and weak to move or talk.

"I wish you'd never built this thing," Mr. Shaw tells Dad.

Finally I wake up and the cramps are gone. Dad hands me a cup of water, and I gulp it down. Most of the others are awake. Somehow they don't look as sick as before.

"It's time," says Mr. McGovern. His jaw is covered by a short, scruffy beard, and the skin that once stretched tightly over his round belly is loose and saggy.

"Let me check—" Dad begins to reach for the radiation kit.

"I don't care anymore," Mr. McGovern says, cutting him short. "I'm going up."

He doesn't sound crazy or desperate like Mr. Shaw did. Instead, he's calm and determined. When he starts to get up, I half expect Dad to try and stop him, but he doesn't. Paula watches without a word.

Mr. McGovern stands in the dim shadows, a grown, naked man with skinny legs and flat feet. "I'll need the light," he says.

Dad picks up the flashlight.

"Can I come?" Sparky asks.

"No."

"Please?"

"Make sure he stays there," Dad tells Janet, and takes out two of the gas masks.

With the masks on, they look like naked men with horse heads. The shelter gets darker when Dad follows Mr. McGovern around the shield wall and into the narrow corridor. We listen to the muffled sounds of Mr. McGovern's grunts and heavy breaths as he starts to climb up the rungs. Then it gets quiet. Then more grunts and heavy breaths. Another quiet period follows.

Finally the bolt beneath the trapdoor slides open with a screech.

My heart speeds up.

Silence.

Then a grunt and a groan as if Mr. McGovern is struggling.

"It's heavy," Dad says, his voice muffled by the mask.

A louder groan follows, along with the clank of metal.

Then more heavy breathing.

We all hear what Mr. McGovern says next: "There's something on the other side blocking it."

A sense of alarm spreads. Mr. and Mrs. Shaw push themselves up and go see. The rest of us follow. Soon we've all squeezed into the narrow corridor watching while Mr. McGovern climbs down the rungs. Dad hands him the flashlight, then turns and looks at us through his mask. Is he going to tell us to go back into the shelter? No. He starts to climb.

Above him is the trapdoor. This is the first time I've seen it since the night we came down here, and back come all the awful memories of the struggle and the desperate cries of those above who didn't get in. Dad was right. Of all the things that have happened, those horrible sounds and haunting pleas are still what I remember most clearly. And somehow, even though I'm only eleven, I know they'll follow me forever.

Dad has to stop partway up the rungs to catch his breath. *Come on,* I think anxiously. *Hurry!*

He starts to climb again, then places his hand against the trapdoor and pushes up. The door rises a fraction of an inch and then falls closed with a loud *clank!* He tries again, straining, and the door rises a tiny bit higher before falling. Dad lowers himself a rung and stares up, catching his breath. Even though he's been weakened by lack of food and exercise, he should have been able to push the trapdoor open.

Mrs. Shaw says what's on all our minds: "We're trapped."

fifty

When Mr. Kasman asked if we'd watched the president on TV, Paula's hand shot up. "He ordered the navy to stop the Russians from giving missiles to Cuba."

"And now what happens?"

I raised my hand. "We wait to see whether the Russian ships will turn back or keep going."

"What will happen if they don't turn back?"

I raised my hand again. "It could be war."

The class grew quiet. Was everyone thinking that the sirens might start at any moment? That right at this very second, Khrushchev could be ordering an attack? That Russian bombers might already be on their way and missiles could be blasting off?

Dickie Keller raised his hand. "My father says we should bomb them before they bomb us."

"But what if they don't really intend to attack us?" asked Mr. Kasman.

Eric Flom raised his hand. "Then why are they putting missiles on Cuba?"

"Some people think it's because we have missiles in Turkey aimed at them."

"We do?" Freak O' Nature asked in his normal voice, sounding surprised.

Mr. Kasman pulled down a map of Europe and eastern Asia and used a wooden pointer. "Turkey is almost the same distance to Moscow as Cuba is to Washington."

Dickie Keller raised his hand. "Why did we put missiles there?"

"I'd guess for the same reason that the Russians are putting missiles on Cuba," Mr. Kasman answered.

"To attack them?" Eric Flom asked, reflecting the confusion many of us felt. Could this really be true? On TV, President Kennedy had said we wanted peace, not war, and that we would never attack Russia unless they attacked us first.

"Does that change the way you think about the situation?" Mr. Kasman asked.

Maybe it was still too early in the morning. Or maybe this information was too confusing, but we sat there like bumps on a log. The room would have been completely silent were it not for a faint scratching sound. Mr. Kasman frowned, then stepped quietly toward the back. We all turned to watch.

Puddin' Belly Wright's head lay on his arm as if he were asleep, but he wasn't. He was busy scratching his initials into the scratch-proof desktop with a paper clip. Mr. Kasman tiptoed close and craned his neck. After a moment, Puddin' Belly must have sensed that it was too quiet. He straightened up with an astonished expression when he realized that we were all watching him, then quickly placed his forearm over his handiwork.

"Move your arm, Stuart."

Puddin' Belly slid it away, revealing the initials SW scratched nearly a quarter of an inch into the new desktop. Everybody held their breath and waited for Mr. Kasman to send him to the office, where Principal Sharp would probably suspend him and make his parents pay for a new desk.

"Looks like you've been working pretty hard, Stuart," said our teacher. "Imagine what would happen if you applied all that energy to your schoolwork."

Puddin' Belly hung his head remorsefully.

Mr. Kasman patted him on the shoulder. "Think about it, okay?"

51

"We're not trapped," Dad says as he climbs down the rungs.

"How can you say that?" Mr. McGovern demands.

"The door moved. We just have to get whatever's on top of it off."

"And how, if I may ask, do you plan to do that?" Paula's dad asks.

"Give me a moment, okay?" Dad grumbles.

"Lot of good *that* will do us," Mr. McGovern mutters.

Sparky kicks Mr. McGovern in the leg. My brother's not strong enough to hurt him with his bare foot, but Mr. McGovern jumps and looks surprised.

"Edward!" Dad snaps.

But I think, *Good for you, Sparky.*

Are we doomed to slowly starve to death in this dark, damp, smelly dungeon?

Dad goes back into the shelter and sweeps the flashlight around until it stops on the bunk bed next to the one where Mom lies. "Steven, could you give me a hand?" he asks.

"To do what?" Mr. Shaw replies.

"Take the bunk apart and put it back together on the other side," Dad says. "Then we can stand on it and push open the trapdoor."

It sounds like a lot of work, and I'm surprised when Mr. Shaw, who acts like everything is so hopeless, agrees to help.

Dismantling the bunk takes time. Dad gets tired and has to rest. Mr. Shaw takes over for a while, and then Mrs. Shaw, and even Mr. McGovern. Parts have to be unscrewed, then moved around the shield wall and put back together. With the extra activity, the air gets stale faster, so Dad assigns Ronnie and me to crank the ventilator. They need to use the flashlight, so when they're working on the other side of the shield wall, the rest of us are in near-dark.

"We should eat what's left," says Mr. McGovern,

panting as he finishes assembling part of the bunk. "There's no point in rationing anymore."

It takes a moment to realize what he means: if we really are trapped down here, rationing what food is left isn't going to make a difference. My heart rises into my throat, and I try to swallow it down. Imagine running out of food, then growing weaker and weaker until no one has the strength to crank the ventilator. . . .

"It could still take a while to get out," Dad cautions.

"You men should eat," suggests Mrs. Shaw. "It will help give you the strength you'll need to get this done."

"I feel terrible doing this," Dad says a little later, running his finger around the inside of the peanut butter jar to get every last smudge. But the strange thing is, it isn't so hard to watch. I've been hungry for so long that I've almost gotten used to it. What's more upsetting is knowing that after this there'll be no more food no matter what happens.

"You're doing it for our sake," Mrs. Shaw reminds him.

It doesn't take long for the men to finish what little food is left, but rather than get back to work, they yawn and say they have to rest first.

So we wait while they nap. But it's hard because now the clock is ticking. The food's gone. If we don't get out soon, we'll really begin to starve.

fifty-two

We continued to do normal stuff at school, but it felt like a shadow hung over everything. You couldn't forget about the Russians for long. A teacher would pull down a shade, and you'd think about how Puddin' Belly was supposed to do that if we were attacked. Or a kid would slam a locker, and everyone in the hall would jump.

On the news, they talked about the Russian ships sailing toward Cuba and the American blockade around the island. The moment of confrontation was nearing.

At dinnertime, Sparky and I went into the kitchen and found Mom sitting at the table, gazing out at the backyard.

"Where's Dad?" Sparky asked.

"Working late."

"Because there might be a war?" I asked.

Mom puffed on her cigarette. "I don't know."

"Is there any news?" I asked.

She blinked, and I could see that she wasn't certain what I meant.

"About the Russians?" I added.

"I haven't been listening."

That seemed strange. Why wasn't she following the news like everyone else?

"What's for dinner?" Sparky asked. Mom glanced at the kitchen clock, then got up and looked in the refrigerator. She said dinner would be ready soon and we should go watch TV.

While Sparky watched and Mom cooked, I snuck into my parents' bedroom. Inside the top drawer of Dad's dresser was a felt-lined tray with compartments for cuff links, tie tacks, and tie bars. Dad had a miniature gold tennis-racket tie bar and a silver one that was a pair of crossed skis. Another compartment held the small brass stays he inserted into his shirt collars so that they would keep their shape all day.

The next drawer contained Dad's shirts, each one folded over a piece of cardboard and held in place by a paper band. The mixed scents of Dad's body smell and chemicals from the dry cleaner wafted up as I slid my hands under the stacks of shirts and felt around. The drawer below that one contained underwear — white V-necked T-shirts and boxers. The bottom drawer was for sweaters.

I tried his closet next. Here amid the hanging suits and slacks, the scent of feet and leather filled my nostrils. Two shelves held shoes, each pair kept in its proper shape by wooden shoe trees. A small chest of drawers contained Dad's wool socks, tennis clothes, and sweatshirts. I slid my hands under the contents. Nothing. So Ronnie was wrong. Not every father hid *Playboy* in his dresser drawers.

Now I looked up. Above the rod where Dad's suits hung was a shelf, and from the floor I could see the corners of things like boxes and maybe a book. I climbed up on the chest of drawers. The shelf was still mostly out of reach, but if I stretched on my tiptoes, there was one green box I was able to work toward the edge until it tipped and fell into my hands. It was the size of a cereal box but heavy, and I was lucky that it didn't slip through my fingers and crash to the floor.

The box had the shiny, slick feel of newness. Still standing on the chest of drawers, I opened it curiously.

Inside was a gun.

Other than on a policeman's belt, it was the first real gun I'd ever seen. The metal had a vague sheen of oil, and I was afraid to touch it, afraid that it might go off accidentally in my hands.

Then Mom called: "Scott? Edward? Dinner!"

I inched the box back up on the shelf. There was only one reason why Dad would have a gun: for war.

In the kitchen, instead of setting the table, Mom had placed two plates of spaghetti and meatballs on a tray, along with napkins, forks, and glasses of milk.

She said, "They're for you and Edward. Go eat in the den."

"Dad said we're not allowed."

"I say you can," Mom said.

I carried the tray into the den, where Sparky was watching *Quick Draw McGraw*, and placed the food between us.

Sparky touched the spaghetti with his fork, then stared at the TV. I felt my insides tighten anxiously. Dad had a gun. Mom was letting us eat in the den. Could there be any clearer signs that the end of the world was approaching?

53

We sit in near-dark in the shelter and listen while the men work on the other side of the shield wall. Sparky has taken up permanent residence on Janet's lap.

"What's the first thing you'll do when you get out?" Mrs. Shaw asks.

Sparky: "Everything."

Paula: "Take a bath."

Ronnie: "Eat something good."

Me: "Take a bath *and* eat something good."

Ronnie's mom says, "What about you, Janet?"

"Look for my children, Mrs. Shaw."

Ronnie's mom utters a little "Oh!" of surprise. "I'm so sorry."

As if there weren't already a million reasons to feel bad, now I feel even worse. The two small faces at the window the day Mom drove Janet home . . . All the time we've been together down here, she never said a word. Sparky snuggles closer to her. "If you can't find them, you can be my other mommy."

Janet starts to cry.

The fathers' voices come around the shield wall. "Move it a little to the right." "Can you shine the light on this?" "Anyone see the screwdriver?"

Finally Dad calls, "I think we're ready."

We go into the corridor to find the bunk bed rebuilt under the trapdoor. Standing on the floor, Mr. McGovern is holding the flashlight on Dad and Mr. Shaw, both wearing masks and squatting naked on the top bunk under the trapdoor. Dad presses his back against it. He reminds me of that statue in New York City of Atlas holding up the world, only Atlas was all muscles and Dad looks so skinny. Next to him, Mr. Shaw lies on his back with his feet against the door.

They grit their teeth and push and strain. The bunk bed creaks; the trapdoor rises slowly. The creaking grows louder.

The trapdoor rises a tiny bit more.

Crack! The sound of splintering wood explodes into our ears.

"Stop!" Mr. Shaw gasps.

Clank! The trapdoor slams down.

Atop the bunk, both fathers breathe hard for a moment, then Dad asks, "What happened?"

"The board under us cracked," says Mr. Shaw.

"Of course," Mr. McGovern says, as if he's just realized something. "You're pushing up on a metal door, but at the same time you're pushing down on a wooden board. This is never going to work."

fifty-four

The Russian ships were getting closer to the quarantine line set up by the United States Navy. There was going to be a showdown. Would one side back down, or would there be war?

My stomach was in a nonstop knot, and I would catch myself at my school desk with my hands clenched and my toes curled up in my shoes. At lunch, the spaghetti and meatballs looked slimy, and I hardly had any appetite anyway. On the way home from school, I asked Ronnie if he wanted to play Nok-Hockey again.

"Why?" He asked.

"Don't you want a rematch?"

"I killed you last time."

"You won't this time."

Ronnie gave me an uncertain look.

"Scared I'll win?" I challenged him.

He snorted. "Fat chance."

We went to his house, where he beat me eleven games to one.

"Can I eat over?" I asked. "We could watch TV."

The Shaws were the only family I knew with a color television set. In the den, Ronnie and I watched *The Jetsons,* but what I really wanted to do was look in a *Playboy* before we went to war, only I was afraid Ronnie would make fun of me. When *The Jetsons* ended, Ronnie glanced toward the kitchen, where his mom had started dinner, and then went to the liquor cabinet and poured some Dubonnet into a glass. "We'll share," he whispered.

We each drank some, and then Ronnie went to the bathroom to wash the glass. As soon as he left the den, I lifted the bottle of Dubonnet to my lips and took a big gulp. The wine warmed my throat and my empty stomach, and I felt myself relax. The anxiety of war became one step removed.

Ronnie and I watched more TV. A little while later, Mr. Shaw came into the den wearing a suit and smelling of cigarettes and the train. He looked serious. "Any news?"

We shook our heads.

Ronnie's dad took off his jacket and rolled up his

sleeves. "How about a little something to take the edge off, gentlemen?"

Ronnie and I shared an uncertain look.

"Come on, boys, you wouldn't let a man drink alone at a time like this, would you?"

It wasn't long before I had a glass filled with ice and more Dubonnet. Ronnie shot me a smirk as if he thought we were getting away with something. Little did he know.

We sipped our drinks. When I closed my eyes, I felt like I was on the deck of a boat in swaying seas.

"That bomb shelter might come in handy after all, Scott," Mr. Shaw said. For once he wasn't joking.

"You really think we could go to war, Dad?" Ronnie asked.

"It's hard to imagine," Mr. Shaw said gravely. "I mean, the sheer insanity of it. No one can win."

"What if the Russians don't care about winning?" Ronnie asked.

Mr. Shaw sighed and shook his head.

From the kitchen, Mrs. Shaw called, "Dinner's ready. I called your mom, Scotty. She said it was okay."

Mr. Shaw got up. "Shall we?"

I stood up, and the room suddenly rocked.

55

"It's hopeless," mumbles Mr. Shaw.

We're all back in the shelter. Mom's on her bunk. The rest of us sit on chairs or on the floor.

"Is it, Dad?" Sparky asks.

"I need to think," Dad says.

"About what?" Mr. McGovern demands. "How stupid it was to build this shelter in the first place? How much better it would have been if we'd just died when we had the chance?"

"*Shut up!*" Dad shouts so loudly, we all jump. This time, Paula's father does what Dad says.

I'm scared sick. The shelter seems dimmer than usual until Dad replaces the batteries in the flashlight and it's brighter again.

"Well, at least you made sure to have enough batteries," Mr. McGovern says bitterly.

"Buried alive," Mr. Shaw mutters.

Sparky lets out a frightened whimper and hugs Janet tightly.

"There's a way," Dad says a little while later.

"Oh, give it up already, will you?" Mr. McGovern growls.

"What's your idea?" asks Mrs. Shaw.

"We have to reinforce the bunk bed."

"It won't work," Mr. McGovern says.

Dad turns to Mr. Shaw as if asking if he'll help, but Ronnie's dad lowers his head.

They don't think it can be done. And if they won't help, it's hopeless. Dad can't do it alone. My insides churn. How can they just give up and let us die down here?

It's Janet who speaks up. "I'll help you, Mr. Porter. I want to find my children."

Her eyes meet Dad's, and he blinks slowly and hard as if to fight back tears. Is it because he's grateful that she's offered to help? Or is it sadness because it's hard to imagine how her children could still be alive?

"Thank you," Dad says.

They begin by moving Mom from her bunk to some pillows on the floor and making her comfortable. Then Dad turns toward the bunk she was lying on and says, "We have to take this one apart and use the pieces to reinforce the other one." But his shoulders stoop, as if just the thought of all that work is too much. "We're going to need more hands."

None of the other grown-ups reply.

I clear my throat. "I'll help."

"Me, too," says Sparky.

Dad gives us a weak smile as if he doesn't think we can make much of a difference. You can tell by the way he looks at Mr. Shaw that he's hoping he'll try again, but Ronnie's father sits besides his wife with his knees pulled up under his chin and doesn't respond.

"What good will giving up do?" Dad asks.

Ronnie's dad looks up at him, and then back down without answering.

"Seriously, Steven," Dad persists.

"I don't know what's on the other side of that trapdoor, but whatever it is, it's too heavy," Mr. Shaw finally says. "We tried, Richard. Before the board cracked."

Dad stands still, his face tilted upward in thought. Is he considering giving up, too?

He looks at Sparky and me. "I'm going to keep trying. Come on, boys."

I realize I've been holding my breath. When I push

myself up, dizziness causes my vision to narrow, and I have to bend over with my hands on my knees and my head as low as it will go.

When I straighten up, everyone's staring.

"You okay?" Dad whispers.

I nod. He gives me a screwdriver and shows me which screws to take out of Mom's bunk bed. I do what I'm told, but I don't say what I'm really wondering: Is he just trying to keep us busy so we won't think about what's ahead?

fifty-six

"Whoa!" In the Shaws' den, Ronnie's father caught me by the arm. "Steady, sailor."

Holding my elbow, he led me into the kitchen, where four aluminum trays were set with little compartments that kept the meat from touching the potatoes and vegetables. Mrs. Shaw pointed to a chair. "You're there, Scotty."

I went to sit but missed the chair and nearly fell over. Mrs. Shaw frowned and looked at her husband.

"Cheap drunk," said Mr. Shaw.

Mrs. Shaw's eyes widened. "Steven, you didn't."

"Couldn't have been more than a thimbleful," Mr. Shaw said. "He just needs to get something in his stomach."

We began to eat. I tried to cut into the meat, but it was really tough.

"Ahem, Scott." Mr. Shaw cleared his throat. "Your knife's upside down."

"Oh." I turned the knife and started again. That's when the Salisbury steak shot off my tray and landed in the middle of the table like a small brown island on a sea of white.

"Let's try a sharper knife." Mr. Shaw went to a drawer and got one with a black handle. "Careful with this one, okay? We'd like to send you home with all ten fingers."

Ronnie made a funny noise, as if muffling a laugh. I decided to try the corn, but most of the kernels fell off the fork before they got to my mouth.

"Care to spoon-feed your friend, Ronnie?" Mrs. Shaw suggested.

"Why doesn't he just go home?" Ronnie sounded like I'd become an embarrassment. His parents had a conversation with their eyes.

Mr. Shaw turned to me. "Try the mashed potatoes, Scott."

It would have been impolite not to, but as soon as I felt that mealy sensation in my mouth, I spit them back onto the tray.

Ronnie muttered, "Jesus Christ."

"Sorry," I apologized. "I forgot that I hate mashed potatoes."

"*Now* will you send him home?" Ronnie begged his parents. "Or are you scared you'll get into trouble because he's drunk?"

"He's not drunk," Mrs. Shaw replied.

"Oh, really?" Ronnie asked in a fresh way that would have definitely gotten me spanked. "What would you call it?"

57

I can't loosen the bunk-bed screws. Are they *that* tight, or have I just grown too weak? I'm so scared that we're never going to get out, but I keep it to myself because I don't want to make things worse. Paula quietly weeps and clings to her dad. Sparky tried to help but gave up and now huddles with Janet, his eyes nervous and darting.

Ronnie takes the screwdriver and tries, but he can't get the screws loose, either. Dad struggles with them for a while, then gives up and sits down beside Janet, Sparky, and me. He gazes away, slowly kneading the muscles in his forearms. "I'm sorry, Janet."

She places her hand on his shoulder. "Take a rest and try again, Mr. Porter," she gently urges him. "For your children. For mine."

Dad lets out a deep sigh, then picks up the screwdriver and tries again.

A hand gently shakes me awake. It's Dad. He's finally gotten one of the bunk boards loose and needs help carrying it around the shield wall.

I yawn and get up, and we carry the board into the narrow corridor. Dad looks up at the bunk, and once again his shoulders sag as if he's not sure he has the strength to lift the board up there. We lean against the cinder blocks. Everyone else is on the other side of the shield wall. Dad puts his arms around me, and I slide mine around his waist and press my cheek against his cool skin. I think he must be a good father. There may have been a lot of things he didn't think of, and a lot of times he got mad and spanked Sparky and me, but he was never mean.

And he always tried his best.

When we go back into the shelter, it feels like no one's moved. Dad starts to unscrew another bunk board but spends more time resting than working. Janet kneads his shoulders and whispers encouragement. When he's finally ready to move the second board, he asks her to help. The three of us pick it up and take a few steps, but the board slips out of our hands and hits the floor with a loud *clack!* Everyone jumps.

"Listen," Dad says, breathing hard. "We can't do this without the rest of you." He pauses as if just the act of talking takes an effort. "If you folks just want to sit here and wait for the end, I can't stop you. But I want to keep trying."

No one moves. The air is stale. The ventilator should probably be cranked.

"You're wasting your time," says Mr. McGovern. "Whatever's on top of the door is too heavy."

"No one's going to come and save us, Herb," Dad answers. "This is our only chance."

No one moves.

We sit. Dad hugs Sparky and me to him. I touch Sparky's arm and nod over at Janet. He may only be nine, but he knows what I'm thinking. He takes her hand.

What a good little brother he is.

In the dim light, Ronnie sits between his parents, holding their hands. Mr. McGovern has his arm around Paula. Everyone's quiet — lost in thought, I guess. My thoughts go to my friends. I think about playing fungo and touch football and throwing dirt bombs and burning leaves. How could they do this to kids? We never had anything against Russian kids, and it's hard to believe they had anything against us.

What'd we do to deserve this?

"May I say something, Mr. Porter?" Janet's voice squeezes through the gloom.

"Yes, of course, Janet."

She addresses everyone. "Mr. and Mrs. Shaw, Mr. McGovern, if we die in here, you'll go to your graves knowing what happened to your children."

Heads rise as they exchange quizzical looks.

"As awful as this is, you'll have that peace of mind," Janet continues. "Without your help, I will never know what happened to mine."

Silence.

"Please," Janet urges them. "I am asking you to put yourself in my place."

Silence.

fifty-eight

"The Yankees sure are something, huh?" Mr. Shaw said after dinner. "Four World Series in seven years."

"Yeah." I'd managed to eat most of the steak and corn. The euphoric feeling brought on by the wine was gradually giving way to throbbing in my skull.

"Maybe this'll be the Giants' year to win it all, too."

"Definitely," I said. "Tittle's great."

"He your favorite player?"

"No, Sam Huff."

"A fine linebacker," Mr. Shaw agreed. "Your dad taking you to any games this fall?"

I started to shake my head, but that made it hurt more. Dad was a football fan, but we'd never gone to a game.

"Ronnie and I go a lot," Mr. Shaw said. "Have a great time, don't we, Sport?"

Ronnie nodded morosely.

"Maybe you'd like to come with us to a game?"

"You mean, if there isn't a war?" I asked.

"That's right," Mr. Shaw said patiently. "We'll only go to the game if we haven't gone to war. Would you like that, Scott?"

"Sure, that would be great," I said.

Ronnie's dad smiled. "Okay, let's plan on it."

When it was time to go, Ronnie got his jacket.

"Where are you going?" I asked.

"With you."

"Because I'm drunk?" I asked.

Mr. Shaw rubs my head. "You're not drunk, Scott. Now, run along."

It was dark and chilly outside. Ronnie kicked a stone down the sidewalk. "Don't tell your parents, okay?"

"That I'm going to a football game?"

"No, dummy, about the wine." He held up his pinkie. "Swear?"

I had to think about it. I guess I knew they were using the Giants to get me to not tell, but the truth was, except for my head hurting, no harm had been done. I didn't know why I'd taken that big gulp of Dubonnet, but they hadn't made me, and I didn't want to get the Shaws into trouble or to make Ronnie angry with me.

I hooked my pinkie to his. "Swear."

"Okay." He nodded grimly and patted me on the back. "See you tomorrow."

59

No one's spoken since Janet made her plea for their help to find her children. I know they must feel as bad as I do, but right now we're so weak, and fortifying the broken bunk bed under the trapdoor seems like such a huge task. Maybe if we just rest awhile . . .

But minutes pass and no one moves.

It's Sparky who finally speaks up. "I'll try again, Janet."

Of course, there's nothing he can do, but somehow, hearing him say it gets the others to reconsider. Eventually, everyone, even Mr. McGovern, agrees to try. It takes a while, but we manage to get the boards up on top of the bunk under the trapdoor. Dad wants to use some of the posts from the other bunk bed to make this one stronger, and Mr. McGovern suggests angling them in a way that Dad didn't think of.

Sometimes it feels like we're working in slow motion, but finally we're ready.

Then Dad climbs up and says something that really surprises me: "Ronnie and Scott, I want you to help. There's only room for two adults up here. But I think we can squeeze two boys in place of one adult and still have room for me."

As frightening as it all is, it makes me feel good that Dad wants me to help. That he thinks Ronnie and me together will be stronger than Mr. Shaw.

We slowly climb up on the reinforced bunk bed, and all three of us put on gas masks. Feeling a crazy mixture of fright and hope, I lie on my back next to Ronnie with our feet against the underside of the cold trapdoor while Dad wedges his back against it. "I hate to say it, boys, but our lives depend on this."

What if I'm not strong enough?

What if no one would be strong enough?

"One, two, three . . . push!"

We grimace and push as hard as we can. It's difficult to breathe with the masks on, and the clear plastic disks quickly fog from exertion. The trapdoor feels like it weighs a ton. Something really heavy must be on top of it.

Dad grunts. My heart thuds so hard, I can feel the pulse thumping in my ears. The door rises slightly.

"It's working!" Mrs. Shaw's voice reaches my ears. "Keep going!"

"You can do it!" Sparky yells.

The trapdoor rises a little more. Bright light begins to seep in.

"A post!" Dad croaks, and Mr. Shaw quickly jams one into the gap between the trapdoor and the closet floor above.

"Stop pushing," Dad gasps.

Ronnie and I go limp, panting and exhausted from the effort. The light seeping in around the trapdoor feels unnaturally bright, and we have to squint.

With the light comes cold air. Dad studies the instruments from the radiation kit. "Fifty-five roentgens. That's close enough."

When he yanks off his mask, it catches me off-guard. It almost seems reckless.

"Come on, boys," he urges.

Ronnie and I pull off our masks, and cool, fresh air fills our lungs. It feels amazing.

But with it comes a smell.

Like rotten meat.

The others smell it. Noses wrinkle, eyes wince. Dad's face falls. "Everyone into the other room," he orders grimly.

Janet leads Sparky back around the shield wall. Ronnie and I climb down and follow. Only the dads stay behind.

In the shelter, Ronnie, Paula, and I sit together, listening to every sound and whisper that comes around the shield wall. Wood scrapes and men grunt.

"Can you turn that post sideways?"

"Wedge it in as far as it will go."

"There's a hammer in the toolbox," Dad says.

Mr. McGovern comes back into the shelter. He seems full of energy, and I wonder whether it's from excitement or if he really has been saving it up like he said he was. He gets the hammer and goes back through the gap, and soon we hear banging.

"That should work."

"What about this piece?"

"Can you jam it in that way?"

A long silence follows. Those of us in the shelter exchange uncertain glances.

"Dad?" I call.

"Just a second," he calls back. Then to the other fathers: "Ready?"

We hear grunts and heaving noises. Wood creaks. Metal hinges squeak. . . .

There's a slithering sound as if something is sliding off the trapdoor.

The narrow corridor on the other side of the shield

wall fills with light. Different light. Natural light. Sparky jumps to his feet and dashes out.

The rest of us follow.

Above us, the trapdoor is open. Dad's standing on top of the bunk bed, his body half out of the shelter, his pale skin bathed in light. It's cold, and the rotten meat smell is awful. Mr. McGovern and Mr. Shaw are standing on the floor below.

"How is it?" Mr. McGovern asks somberly.

Something in Dad's throat catches. "It's . . . okay . . . I guess."

sixty

It was Why Can't You Be Like Johnny?'s birthday. Earlier in the day, a U.S. Air Force spy plane was shot down over Cuba, and now the U.S. Armed Forces were being mobilized. Preparations for war had begun.

The Sinclairs canceled the birthday party but invited Ronnie, Freak O' Nature, and me over for cake because we lived so close. Dad said it was okay to go. This was the first time we'd been allowed in the Sinclairs' house since the Pee Steam Incident of the previous summer. Why Can't You Be Like Johnny?'s bedroom was upstairs and had its own porch, and one night we'd brought sleeping bags over and slept on the porch under the stars. It was chilly in the morning, and Ronnie said that instead of using the bathroom, we should pee over the railing because when it was cold, your pee had steam. Why Can't You Be Like Johnny? said it wasn't cold enough for pee steam, and Ronnie said, "Wanna bet?"

I was surprised that Why Can't You Be Like Johnny? took the bet, but I guess he was determined to prove Ronnie wrong. We stood at the railing and peed down onto the flower beds. Of course, Why Can't You Be Like Johnny? was right because he was always right. Then Ronnie laughed and said he'd known all along that it wasn't cold enough for pee steam and he'd really just wanted to see if he could get us all to pee off the porch.

Unfortunately, Mrs. Sinclair was in the kitchen making breakfast when she looked out the window and saw four glittering gold streams cascading down onto her rosebushes. We were immediately sent home.

"How come she changed her mind?" Freak O' Nature asked while he, Ronnie, and I walked over for birthday cake.

"Maybe she figures we could all be dead tomorrow, so what does it matter?" Ronnie said.

Mrs. Sinclair let us in with a narrow-eyed look as if warning that if we did anything wrong this time, we would be banned from her house forever. The funny thing about the Sinclairs was that they weren't all brains like Why Can't You Be Like Johnny? Mr. Sinclair owned a plumbing company and spent most evenings watching TV. And a few months before, Why Can't You Be Like Johnny?'s eight-year-old sister, Barbara, had swallowed a safety pin and had to go to the hospital.

Mrs. Sinclair served a cake with a rocket ship made of icing, and we sang "Happy Birthday," only under his breath, Ronnie sang:

"Happy birthday to you.
You live in a zoo.
You look like a monkey,
And you smell like one, too!"

I was afraid Mrs. Sinclair had heard him, but she smiled while she cut the rocket cake, so it looked like we were in the clear.

Then Mr. Sinclair brought out a long box wrapped in birthday paper, and Why Can't You Be Like Johnny? got excited because inside was a telescope, and he said we should all go up to his porch and look through it. As we headed upstairs, Mrs. Sinclair once again gave Ronnie, Freak O' Nature, and me that look that said we were dead if we got into any mischief.

Out on the porch, Why Can't You Be Like Johnny? set up the telescope. I felt my insides corkscrew when I imagined looking through it and seeing Russian missiles streaking our way.

He aimed the telescope at the moon. "That big white

spot is Copernicus crater. And that round dark area right above it? That's called the Mare Imbrium. It's Latin for 'the Sea of Rains.'"

"It rains on the moon?" said Freak O' Nature.

"It was a sea of lava," explained Why Can't You Be Like Johnny? "A long time ago, a huge asteroid hit the surface and made a hole so deep that lava came out."

"What's an asteroid?" Freak O' Nature asked.

"It's like a shooting star," said Johnny. "Only it's just a big space rock. People used to think they were stars because they glowed when they burned up in the atmosphere."

I looked up into the dark. A tiny, starlike dot was moving slowly across the night sky. "Like that?" I pointed.

"Oh, my gosh!" Johnny gasped excitedly. "It's *Echo*! The communications satellite."

"You can see it?" Ronnie asked, dubiously.

"It's a giant silver balloon," said Johnny. "This is unreal!"

What was unreal was seeing Johnny get so excited. He never acted like this.

"How do you know it's not a shooting star?" asked Freak O' Nature.

"They streak across the sky and are gone in an instant," said Johnny.

"And how do you know it's not *Sputnik*?" asked Ronnie. *Sputnik* was a Russian satellite.

"You can't see *Sputnik*," said Why Can't You Be Like Johnny? "Here, everyone look."

We took turns looking at *Echo* through the telescope. It still looked like a bright dot, only bigger.

"You know that the Ruskies sent *Sputnik* into space to prove they had a rocket strong enough to launch a nuclear bomb at us?" said Ronnie, looking at me. "Think your bomb shelter can stand up to that, Scott?"

"Pretty soon it won't even matter," said Johnny as we watched *Echo* creep across the star-speckled sky. "Now that we can put men in space, they're going to build laser cannons that can destroy a whole city with a single blast."

I didn't know whether laser cannons were something Johnny had read about in his Tom Swift books or something real, and I didn't want to ask because I was afraid I'd look dumb. Besides, what difference would it make? Why did they need laser cannons when they already had nuclear bombs that could destroy everything? All I knew was that for an instant, while looking at *Echo,* I'd managed to forget about war, but now it had all come rushing back.

High above us, *Echo* gradually dimmed and vanished into the dark.

"Where'd it go?" asked Freak O' Nature.

"Into Earth's shadow," said Johnny.

We watched the sky for something else exciting to come along, but nothing did. Behind us, Ronnie was peering through the telescope. Only it was pointed across the street.

"What are you doing?" asked Johnny.

"Nothing," Ronnie answered.

Why Can't You Be Like Johnny? aimed the telescope at the moon again and showed us some mountains and craters. Then Mrs. Sinclair came out and said it was time to go.

Outside the Sinclairs' house, Freak O' Nature went one way, and Ronnie and I went the other. Bugs zoomed crazily around the streetlights, kind of like missiles.

"Guess what I saw tonight?" Ronnie asked.

"The moon and that *Echo* satellite."

"How about Paula's bedroom?"

"How?"

"With the telescope, dummy. Right into her window. Want to know what I saw?"

I stopped under a streetlight and squinted at him. Here we were possibly on the brink of World War III, and all he could think about was looking in a girl's bedroom. My jaw tightened, and I suddenly felt angry. Maybe because I was so scared and he was acting like he wasn't. "No," I said.

Ronnie put his hands on his hips. "Sure, you do."

"No . . . I . . . don't."

61

Dad looks down from the trapdoor with a pained expression. "Steven, could you climb up here? Herb, would you get everyone back into the shelter, and then come up and join us?"

"But, Dad—" Sparky starts.

"You'll all be out soon," Dad promises. "You just have to wait a little longer."

Mr. McGovern herds us back around the shield wall. His eyes look glittery. In a quavering voice, he says, "Stephanie, make sure the kids stay put."

Janet and Mrs. Shaw stand guard by the shield wall to make sure we don't try to sneak back into the corridor.

You'd think they'd be ecstatic that we can finally get out, but they're both quiet and sad.

"Why can't we go?" Sparky asks.

"Soon, I promise." Mrs. Shaw strokes his head reassuringly.

Sparky looks up into Janet's face. She nods.

Ronnie leans so close, his lips practically touch my ear. "You know what was on top of the door?" he whispers.

"Uh-huh."

Paula's face scrunches up as if she might start to cry. Ronnie reaches out, hesitates, then places his hand on her arm. I watch their eyes meet. "We'll all get out soon," he says, sounding just like my father.

But every second we wait feels like forever. Cold air fills the shelter, and we start to shiver. Finally Dad calls down, "Scott?"

I go into the corridor and squint in the light coming through the square above. Dad's up there, out of the shelter, wearing dungarees and a sweatshirt. "It won't be long," he says, dropping down a box of Ritz crackers and a package of Oreo cookies. "Here's something to keep you busy. They're okay to eat."

Back in the shelter, everyone eats ravenously. Stale crackers and cookies never tasted so good.

sixty-two

"Why not?" Ronnie asked.

Trouble swirled around me like those bugs around the streetlight. It was times like this when I wished Ronnie wasn't my best friend. I needed a friend I could admit I was scared to without having to worry that he'd make fun of me. "Because we might be on the verge of nuclear war. Doesn't that bother you?"

Ronnie shrugged. "Okay, forget it. I'm not gonna tell you what I saw."

"Suit yourself," I said.

Ronnie narrowed his eyes. "Come on, admit it— you're dying to know."

"No, I'm really not," I said, feeling anger and fear and resentment percolating inside me. "And you want to know why? Because we could all be killed tonight. And if we're not, you're gonna come up with some scheme to look through Paula's window again, and I'm gonna get in a ton of trouble. And you're not gonna get in any trouble because you never get punished for anything."

"You are the biggest baby I ever saw," Ronnie taunted. "You don't know anything, and you're afraid to find out. Go be a coward in your dumb bomb shelter. Want to know something? My dad thinks your dad's an idiot. Because there's never gonna be a war because everyone knows the world would be destroyed and no one would win. Only an idiot would be stupid enough to build a bomb shelter."

"Well, your father's stupid for giving kids wine and reading *Playboy* in front of them and never making you do any chores," I shot back. "And your mom's stupid because she dresses like a movie star even though she's just a mother, and she gives you TV dinners instead of real meals because she's too lazy to cook."

"Coward," Ronnie said.

"Spoiled brat," I said.

"Homo."

I balled my hands into fists and swung as hard as I could, hitting him on the arm. It must have hurt a little, but not enough. Ronnie tackled me, and we slammed to the street and rolled around, swinging our fists wildly. I knew I was going to lose, but it didn't matter. I just wanted to hit him as hard as I could. I wanted to make him pay for calling my father an idiot and for not being scared and not doing chores and for always getting me into trouble and having a home filled with so many temptations.

Even when Ronnie pinned me on my back, I still kicked and tried to hit him. If it hadn't been for him, I wouldn't have stolen that cheesecake or drunk too much Dubonnet or had to think about my mother's breasts and queers. I was sure that behind our backs his father made fun of my father, and that his mother was one of the ladies who stared at my mother in the supermarket.

"Break it up. Come on, boys, that's enough." Dad's voice came through the dark.

I felt Ronnie's weight rise off me and saw Dad pulling him by the arm. I pushed myself to my feet. My right elbow stung where the skin had been scraped, and my knee throbbed where I'd banged it on the street.

"What's this about?" Dad asked.

Ronnie and I glared at each other but said nothing. Except for his shirt hanging out and one knee of his pants being torn, he didn't look like he'd even been in a fight.

"Come on, what's the story?" Dad asked.

We were silent. I knew that if I told what happened, I'd be labeled a tattletale and a sissy. Dad probably knew it, too.

"Okay, Ronnie, you better go home." He let go, and Ronnie headed toward his house.

Dad and I started up our driveway, but I limped.

"You okay?" he asked.

"Yeah."

"Want to tell me what happened?"

I shook my head.

"A boy thing, huh?" He smiled slightly, almost as if he was proud.

"Yeah."

Mom cleaned my elbow and knee with Mercurochrome, which stung even more than scraping them had in the first place. She was annoyed when I said I couldn't tell her what had happened and Dad said it was my private business. I had a feeling they were going to have an argument.

I went to bed wondering if Ronnie was right and there wouldn't be a war after all. I wondered what would happen tomorrow when I saw him at the bus stop. Would he tell everyone we'd had a fight? Would he say he won or that it had been broken up before either of us could win?

Dad came in and sat on the side of my bed. "How're you feeling?" he whispered.

I shrugged. It hurt, but not as much as you'd imagine a fight would. "Mom was pretty mad," I said.

"She's been upset about a lot of things lately." Dad seemed sad. "It's a hard time for everyone."

"You think there's going to be a war?"

"No one knows," he answered.

"That's what the fight was about, kind of."

He looked surprised. "Seriously?"

"Ronnie said something bad about you because of the bomb shelter."

Dad let his breath out and slowly nodded. "Maybe they're right. Maybe it was a mistake. I was just trying to protect us."

"I think you did the right thing, Dad."

One of his eyebrows rose. "Even though you got into a fight about it?"

I shrugged. "Ronnie's a jerk."

"But he's your best friend."

"Yeah."

A sad knowing smile crept onto Dad's lips. "Kind of like your mom and me."

63

Dad throws down clothes. Sparky and I find our own things, and the others put on whatever comes closest to fitting. Mrs. Shaw and Janet dress Mom.

A few minutes later, Dad and Mr. Shaw climb back down into the shelter.

"Can we go up?" Sparky asks.

"In a moment." Dad eases Mom to her feet. It's so strange the way she doesn't know us but knows to walk when he leads her. In the narrow corridor, Janet and Mrs. Shaw work with Dad to get her onto the bunk bed. Above them, Mr. McGovern reaches down to help her out.

Paula and Sparky go next.

Then Mrs. Shaw and Janet.

Then Ronnie.

Dad looks down from above. "Your turn, Scott."

I climb up on the bunk bed toward the light and the bad smell. It's slow going because I'm weak and have to pause and rest, but I'm eager and scared, too. Finally I poke my head out. Even though I'm in the playroom closet, it's so bright that I have to squint. The playroom windows have been blasted out, leaving jagged ridges of glass in the frames. The floor is covered with broken glass, small branches, leaves, and toys. The rotten meat smell is strong, and I don't have to ask what the large lumps are that lie under bedsheets here and there. My insides tighten, and the awful thoughts of what it must have been like for those above gnaws at me.

"Don't look," Dad says. "Go outside."

Behind me, Mr. Shaw climbs out of the shelter and hands Dad the flashlight, first-aid kit, the green box, and some other things. Then he and Dad close the trapdoor.

Out in the backyard, the air is cold and fresh. The trees have been stripped bare, and all that remains are stubby, leafless limbs and trunks missing bark on the side that faced the blast. Window screens, tree branches, roof shingles, and sheets of newspapers lie on the ground among the dead leaves and patches of scorched brown grass. The sun is in the west, so for the first time in weeks, we have a sense of what time it is. The air is still, and the sky is mostly blue, with a few feathery clouds here and there.

Up here in the light, it's a shock to see how thin and gaunt everyone's gotten. Dad and Mr. McGovern look strange with their short beards. We move slowly and keep looking upward as if trying to adjust to not having a ceiling overhead. Squinting in the angled sunlight, we hug ourselves, not just because we're chilled.

We're outside.

It's so quiet that we can hear Sparky's teeth chatter.

We're alive.

Squawking and honking comes from overhead. A *V* of black-and-white Canada geese flies high above us.

"From up north," Mr. McGovern says.

"Look." Mr. Shaw points behind us. In the distance a thin column of white smoke rises almost straight up into the air.

"Other people," Dad says.

We're not the only ones.

But now Dad's looking back into the playroom with a stricken expression. He closes his eyes as if he wishes he couldn't see.

Mrs. Shaw takes his arm. "It's horrible, but we all couldn't have survived, Richard."

It's strange that she's the one who says it. Dad nods slowly as if he knows she's right, but it still doesn't make him feel better. He turns to Mr. Shaw and Mr. McGovern. "We have to give them a proper burial."

The others agree. Paula tugs at her father's hand as if there's something he needs to do. "Daddy?"

"Yes, honey, in a second," Mr. McGovern says, and steps closer to Dad. "Steven, I . . ." He trails off and swivels his head at Janet, who looks away. Paula's father turns back to Dad. "I'm sorry. We all made mistakes. . . . Would you watch Paula for me? There are things I need to do."

Dad nods. Mr. McGovern heads off, around our house, toward his own.

Mr. Shaw extends his hand. "Thank you, Richard."

They shake.

"See you in the morning?" Dad asks, tilting his head toward our playroom.

"Yes, definitely."

Mrs. Shaw gives Dad a hug, and Ronnie shakes his hand, then looks at me and moves his lips as if to say, *See you later.* He joins his parents, and they walk across Old Lady Lester's backyard toward their home.

Dad turns to Janet. "It's going to be dark soon. If you can wait until tomorrow, I promise that as soon as we finish what we have to do here, we'll help you look for your children."

"Thank you, Mr. Porter," Janet answers.

When Dad turns to me next and places his hands on

my shoulders, it catches me by surprise. He turns me to face him. "Scott, I'm proud of you. It was terrible down there, and you conducted yourself like a man."

I don't know what to say. Dad smiles and says we should go inside, where he'll make a fire and heat water so we can wash and cook some food. He leads Mom toward the house. Janet and Paula go with him, and I begin to follow, then stop and look back.

Amid the broken branches, torn shingles, and ripped screens, Sparky's on his toes with his arms spread out, spinning around and around on the scorched grass, laughing.

I can't help but smile. What a kid.

AUTHOR'S NOTE

The author, age twelve, with his younger brother, Leigh, standing in front of their family's new below-ground bomb shelter, 1962. A playroom and bedroom would soon be built over the shelter.

The one-story ranch house looks smaller than I remember. The white pine in the front yard that I used to climb as a boy looms a dozen feet higher than the roof. The locust tree I helped my father plant fifty years ago is now almost as tall as the pine. The front lawn, which once felt so expansive, now looks hardly large enough for a game of tag.

The home's current owner invites me in. The slate floor in the living room has been replaced with carpeting, and the kitchen has been modernized. As we walk down the hall toward the back of the house, I am flooded with memories—the games my brother and I played, the fights, the chases, the nooks and crannies we hid in for hide-and-seek.

At the back of the house, where the playroom once was, there is now a short hall and two smaller bedrooms. We go into the first bedroom—decorated in pink, a color virtually nonexistent in the male-dominated home of my childhood—and the owner opens a closet door. He clears away some shoes and dolls from the carpeted floor. "Listen." He raps the carpet with his knuckles, producing a dull, echoing clang. "We never had it removed."

He means the metal trapdoor. He can't show it to me without pulling up the carpet, but it evokes a memory just the same—of the Cuban Missile Crisis and the years after, when the threat of nuclear war had diminished, and the trapdoor practically vanished under toys and balls and other sports equipment.

The trapdoor has been permanently sealed. No one will ever open it and climb down, as I did as a teenager to show my friends the shelter. Instead there is an outside entrance to the shelter now, and, as the owner leads me out to the backyard, he asks me about the stories the neighbors told him when he and his family moved in twenty years ago.

Is it true that before he had the shelter built, my father had a twelve-foot fence erected around the property so that no one would be able to see in? No, I tell him, that's not true. Besides, building a fence would have only invited questions and scrutiny.

Was it true that building the shelter took every spare cent my family had, and as a result we had to forgo vacations, dinners out, and other leisure activities? While I was not privy to my family's finances as a child, it's doubtful. I recall that we vacationed on Cape Cod and skied in Vermont, and we went to Chinese and Italian restaurants.

In the backyard, except for one large weeping willow, the trees I remember are gone. Here concrete steps lead to a subterranean wooden door. Before we descend, the owner tells me the story of having this entrance built: after inspecting the shelter from the inside, the contractor estimated that the job of digging the new outside entrance would take no more than three or four days. At first the digging went quickly, but when the workers started to break through the cinder-block concrete wall, they found something unexpected—an interior lining of quarter-inch-thick iron plating.

A welder had to be brought in to cut through the iron with an acetylene torch, and when this was done, there was yet another surprise—on the other side of the iron plating was a second wall of cinder blocks.

"Your father really wanted to protect you," the owner says as he leads me down the entrance steps.

I wish I could say that once inside the shelter, old, forgotten memories were unearthed, but almost everything down there is different now. The bunks and wooden shelves of supplies are gone, replaced with metal file cabinets. The overhead water tank has been removed, and a dehumidifier hums in one corner. The steel ventilator still pokes out of the wall, but the crank is missing.

Holding a flashlight, the owner leads me around the shield wall and into the narrow corridor beneath the trapdoor. The rungs in the wall are still there, shrouded in spiderwebs. The owner offers an unnecessary apology for the webs, saying he rarely comes down to the shelter anymore, and it has been many years since he's looked on this side of the shield wall.

Later, we leave the shelter and I thank him for allowing me to visit. I get in my car, drive past a few houses, and stop at the top of the hill for which the street is named. Lining the curb are the houses of my childhood friends and neighbors, a few unchanged, but others almost unrecognizable thanks to redesign and renovation. Here my thoughts are once again filled with the memories—of baseball and football games we played on this street, of the Good Humor Man's ringing bells and how we'd all run home to beg our mothers for quarters for ice cream, of playing in piles of leaves, splashing in puddles, and building snowmen. Ours were truly innocent childhoods.

People say that the era of post–World War II American innocence died on November 22, 1963, with the assassination of President John F. Kennedy. But I wonder if perhaps that innocence began to fade earlier than that, with the Cold War nuclear arms race and the threat of mutually assured destruction. Certainly that was the first time my friends and I became aware that there were countries thousands of miles away, on the other sides of vast oceans, that wanted to destroy us. Countries populated by people we didn't know, had never met, and had no reason to dislike.

As history shows, the Cuban Missile Crisis was averted and no bombs fell. The American people were led to believe that Soviet premier Nikita Khrushchev backed down and ordered the ships carrying missiles and other weapons to return to Russia. In actuality, though, the crisis was forestalled when President Kennedy secretly agreed to Khrushchev's demand to remove all American nuclear missiles located in Turkey — on the condition that this information not be made public. Thus, what was presented to our country as a military triumph was at best a draw, if not a defeat.

Why is it that since the dawn of civilization, we have persisted in following a pattern where mere handfuls of influential men manage to convince or force great masses of peaceful human beings to fear and hate one another enough to go to war? Has the result ever been anything other than misery, death, and destruction?

More than fifty years have passed since that week in October of 1962 when the world came the closest it's ever been to complete annihilation. And yet we are still at war.

Will we never learn?

ACKNOWLEDGMENTS

My heartfelt thanks to:

Stephen Barbara, for getting behind this book and steering it to the wonderful folks at Candlewick.

Karen Lotz, for taking a leap of faith on a partial manuscript from an author she'd never worked with before.

And finally, the magnificent Kaylan Adair, whose long, thoughtful, elegantly phrased editorial letters were precious gifts.

QUESTIONS TO CONSIDER

1. *Fallout* is historical fiction, but it rewrites the past. What are the true historical events depicted in this novel? What are the imagined events? Why do you think the author chose to alter the facts of 1962? What do you think he is trying to tell us about the present?

2. The chapters in this novel alternate between the months leading up to the attack and the days immediately following. How does the novel's structure enhance the story's suspense? How does it deepen your understanding of its characters, especially Scott?

3. For half of the twentieth century, the U.S. and the Soviet Union fought each other in the Cold War. What is the difference between a "cold" war and a "hot" one? Which would you rather experience?

4. What is the historical connection between Russia and the Soviet Union? Why do the characters in *Fallout* use both names interchangeably?

5. Before the attack, Mr. Shaw makes fun of the bomb shelter, but afterward he forces himself and his family into it. Do you think he's a hypocrite? What would you have done in his situation?

6. Why was Mrs. Porter opposed to building a bomb shelter? Why does Mr. Porter decide to build it anyway? Before the attack, which parent would you have agreed with? Why?

7. Scott and his classmates often described the Soviet leaders as evil. Why? How did they regard President Kennedy? How did their new teacher, Mr. Kasman, challenge their beliefs?

8. Ronnie could be a liar, a bully, a Peeping Tom, and even on occasion a thief. So why is he Scott's best friend? What happens to their friendship in the shelter?

9. Janet spends one night each week babysitting and cleaning for the Porter family. Why do they know so little about her family?

10. Why does Mr. McGovern want to treat Mrs. Porter and Janet differently from everyone else in the shelter? To him, what makes their lives less valuable? How do the other adults respond to his argument? How would you?

11. For Scott, the worst part of being in the bomb shelter "is the way the grown-ups act" (page 179). What is the difference between the behavior of the children and that of the adults in the shelter? Why can't the adults get along with one another?

12. All the rules of modesty disappear after a few days. "What's the big deal?" Scott wonders (page 187). "Why was it ever a big deal?" How would you answer him? Why does our society value modesty?

13. When Mrs. Shaw predicts a terrifying future for everyone in the shelter, Mr. Porter tries to comfort his worried son. "Things will be different from before," he says (page 122). "But right now we don't know how." What do you think happens to the Porters after the novel ends? How do you imagine your family would be different today if there really had been a nuclear war in 1962?

14. Mr. Porter believes that hope is "all we've got to keep us going" (page 189). Why is hope so powerful? Why doesn't Mr. McGovern trust it?

15. In his author's note, Todd Strasser asks: "Has the result [of war] ever been anything other than misery, death, and destruction?" (page 263). What do you think?